Robin Cummings's Guide to Finding the Perfect Man

—Date Mr. Wrong for two years.

—Call off the wedding with barely a moment to spare. Whew!

—Come to Ranger Springs to lick your wounds and forget about men, then fall into the strong arms of the police chief—who happens to be the most appealing man you've ever met.

—Try to forget about Police Chief Ethan Parker, because you came here to forget about men.

—Fail miserably.

—Realize that Ethan Parker is the perfect man for you, even though it may take the rest of your life to convince *him* you belong together....

Dear Reader,

It's another wonderful month at Harlequin American Romance, the line dedicated to bringing you stories of heart, home and happiness! Just look what we have in store for you....

Author extraordinaire Cathy Gillen Thacker continues her fabulous series THE LOCKHARTS OF TEXAS with *The Bride Said, "Finally!"* Cathy will have more Lockhart books out in February and April 2001, as well as a special McCabe family saga in March 2001.

You've been wanting more books in the TOTS FOR TEXANS series, and author Judy Christenberry has delivered! *The $10,000,000 Texas Wedding* is the not-to-be-missed continuation of these beloved stories set in Cactus, Texas. You just know there's plenty of romance afoot when a bachelor will lose his huge inheritance should he fail to marry the woman he once let get away.

Rounding out the month are two fabulous stories by two authors making their Harlequin American Romance debut. Neesa Hart brings us the humorous *Who Gets To Marry Max?* and Victoria Chancellor will wow you with *The Bachelor Project.*

Wishing you happy reading!

Melissa Jeglinski
Associate Senior Editor

The Bachelor Project

VICTORIA CHANCELLOR

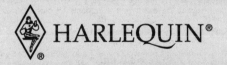

HARLEQUIN®

TORONTO • NEW YORK • LONDON
AMSTERDAM • PARIS • SYDNEY • HAMBURG
STOCKHOLM • ATHENS • TOKYO • MILAN • MADRID
PRAGUE • WARSAW • BUDAPEST • AUCKLAND

To my wonderful in-laws, Lillian & E. V. Huffstutler.
Thank you making me part of the family, and for telling
those great small-town-Texas stories during Sunday
dinner. I love you, Sudie and Dad.

Thanks to former Mineola, Texas, Chief of Police
Jerry Hirsch, and to HGTV for all those great decorating
shows I watch when I should be writing.

ISBN 0-373-16844-6

THE BACHELOR PROJECT

Copyright © 2000 by Victoria Chancellor Huffstutler.

Visit us at www.eHarlequin.com

Printed in U.S.A.

ABOUT THE AUTHOR

While growing up in Louisville, Kentucky, Victoria Chancellor never realized her vivid imagination meant she would someday become a writer. Now married to a Texan and settled in a suburb of Dallas, she thoroughly enjoys creating fictional worlds inhabited by characters who deserve a happy ending. When she's not writing, Victoria cares for her "zoo" of three cats, two ferrets, two tortoises, a flock of naturalized ring-neck doves and assorted wild animals who wander onto her patio for dinner each night. She would love to receive letters at P.O. Box 852125, Richardson, TX 75085-2125. Please enclose a SASE for reply.

Books by Victoria Chancellor

HARLEQUIN AMERICAN ROMANCE
844—THE BACHELOR PROJECT

Don't miss any of our special offers. Write to us at the following address for information on our newest releases.

Harlequin Reader Service
U.S.: 3010 Walden Ave., P.O. Box 1325, Buffalo, NY 14269
Canadian: P.O. Box 609, Fort Erie, Ont. L2A 5X3

All underlined places are fictitious.

Chapter One

There! The scratching, bumping noise filtered through the closed, locked windows.

Robin peered through the mini-blinds into the vast darkness outside the fringe of artificial light. She couldn't see beyond the large pecan trees to the county road. Having grown up in a Houston highrise, she felt as if she were the only person alive in the Texas Hill Country. Of course, there *were* other people around—just not very close. She'd noticed a few other houses, perhaps a quarter-mile away, when she'd driven in early this afternoon.

Floodlights mounted high on the side and back of the residence bathed the lawn and shrubs in a brightness bordering on daylight. Squinting into the shadows, she searched for the source of the suspicious noise she'd heard only moments ago.

Nothing.

She'd hoped to see a wild animal running among the rows of clay pots filled with begonias. Or even a loud car driving carelessly on the two-lane road that connected Ranger Springs to nowhere in particular.

Nothing.

"There's no one outside," she whispered to herself. This comfortable, rural, family home was safe. Her Great-aunt Sylvia's dear friend Bess wouldn't have suggested a town rife with criminals or juvenile delinquents. And certainly no one she knew from Houston would be rummaging around outside the house, especially since they didn't know where she'd run. Why would she tell them, when she didn't want to face family or friends for at least two or three months?

Her hand was poised to turn off the floor lamp in the large den when the sound came again. Horribly clear and menacing, just outside the thin glass windows. Near the dining room? She tilted her head, listening, her body strung tight. No, perhaps the kitchen. She imagined the intruders preparing to enter the house...or maybe just frighten her. Who knew what kind of mischief rural teenagers could perpetrate?

With a frown, she reached for the phone. Was this town large enough to have an emergency number? Somewhere in the house, she'd seen a listing of fire and police departments, but at the moment she couldn't remember where that might be. Well, she'd dial 9-1-1 and see what happened.

"Ranger Springs 9-1-1. What is your emergency?"

"I think I have an intruder. Could you please

send someone out here? I just moved in this afternoon. The house has been empty for a month, and I'm afraid someone might be prowling around.'' Robin swiveled so she could see the windows and listen for more sounds.

"Can you give me a description of the intruder?''

"No, I can't see him…or them. But I heard something just a few minutes ago.''

"What's your address?''

Robin gave the dispatcher the rural route number, but kept on listening for sounds.

"Chief Parker is on his way.''

A horrible crashing noise came from beneath the dining room windows. "Please, hurry,'' she whispered, suddenly more afraid. "I think they're getting desperate.''

"Hold on, ma'am. Tell me your name.''

"Cummings. Robin Cummings. I'm staying at the home of the Franklin family. House-sitting.''

"Chief Parker will be there in just a few minutes. He's on his way. He's listening to the call.''

"Hurry.''

"Do you have a weapon?''

"No,'' Robin said, shuddering as she imagined herself trying to pull the trigger as she stared down the barrel of a pistol. Or, worse yet, clutching a knife to defend herself. "No weapon.''

"I'll be on the line with you until he's there. Stay away from the windows and keep your doors locked until the chief identifies himself.''

"Don't worry,'' Robin said, leaning against the

couch, "everything is locked, and I'm not going anywhere near a door or window."

She pulled her knees up high and hugged them to her chest. The police chief would be here soon. Not just a patrol officer, but The Chief. Someone experienced, mature, competent. She didn't care if he looked like Andy Griffith or the guy Carroll O'Connor had played in that Southern television drama. In just a few minutes, he'd be here and scare the intruders away.

POLICE CHIEF ETHAN PARKER cut the lights on his patrol car; he'd already shut off the siren a ways back. Parking beneath the spreading pecan trees that lined the two-lane blacktop and driveway to the Franklin house, he took just a moment to let his eyes adjust to the darkness so he could look around the property. He seriously doubted that out here in the country there was an intruder lurking in the darkness. More than likely, an animal was scrounging for food or just curious about activity inside the recently vacant home.

Still, he unsnapped the holster restraint and gripped his pistol. Even if a human predator wasn't about this night, he'd seen a couple of pretty large cougars not too far west of here. No sense in tempting fate.

The car's clock reminded him that his shift ended in just ten minutes. If one of his patrol officers wasn't in Austin for a training class, Ethan would be home, getting ready for bed right now. The chief didn't usually work the night shift, but in a small town, every person had to do double duty at times.

He gave his position to Ben, his regular nighttime dispatcher, clipped his call unit on his shoulder, then gripped a flashlight. Ethan eased out of the patrol car into the warm, humid night, shutting the door as silently as possible. Every lamp in the house seemed to be blazing, giving him plenty of light to see around the exterior. Floodlights on two sides illuminated the side and back entrances, and brass fixtures on either side of the ornate front door revealed the wide, deep porch.

Ethan circled the house, listening for any whispers that might indicate some local teens looking for a deserted house to use for a party. Or to sit around outside and drink some beers they'd taken from a parent's refrigerator. Even Ranger Springs wasn't immune to the problems of the city, so he wouldn't put it past a few teens to smoke a little marijuana out here in the country. But the only sounds he heard were the usual summer night noises of crickets and other insects.

A far cry from the career at the FBI he'd given up almost three years ago. Crime in Ranger Springs didn't compare with that in Dallas. In the past three years, he'd never before received a 9-1-1 call from a hysterical woman who feared for her life. He had to wonder who this caller might be—a friend of Mr. and Mrs. Franklin, or someone who'd heard about the vacancy through Gina Mae Summers, the local real estate agent? Ethan had already been making extra patrols to the property just to make sure teens looking for a good hangout hadn't decided an un-inhabited, upscale, three-bedroom house would make a great Party Central.

His boots made barely a sound as they sank lightly into the damp earth. No footprints other than his marked the property, giving him further reas-surance that two-legged predators weren't lurking. Kids weren't nearly as sneaky as they thought they were, and he doubted any one of the teens in Ranger Springs would think to conceal evidence that they'd walked around outside an empty house.

He reached the side entrance, where a couple of moving boxes and some plastic bags tumbled hap-hazardly across the concrete path to the detached garage. Nudging the closer box with his boot, he wasn't too surprised when two dark shapes scram-bled out of the mess. One paused briefly to stand on hind legs and stare at him in curiosity from darkly masked eyes. Then the raccoons both ran to the nearest tree and scurried up the rough bark.

Ethan smiled as he eased his 40-caliber semiau-tomatic into the holster. Reassured that no danger lurked in the moonlit shadows, he approached the front door and knocked.

"Police Chief Ethan Parker," he announced loudly.

He heard the whisper of footsteps, then saw a feminine shape cross the leaded panels. Finally, a woman flung open the heavy oak door.

She stood inside the threshold, dressed in a

skimpy peach-colored robe she clutched around her
middle. Something—perhaps a T-shirt—peeked out
below the hem, brushing against her thighs. Long,
tanned thighs. He took only a second to take in her
average height and build, delicate features and
heart-shaped face and determined she posed no
threat to him.

In the next instant, the description "doe in the
headlights" popped into his head. He'd seen the
same look of fear in large brown eyes just before
he'd slammed on the brakes and steered to avoid
one of the beautiful and plentiful deer that popu-
lated the Hill Country.

"Miss Cummings?" Thankfully, he remembered
her name from the dispatcher's conversation. Every
other rational, professional thought seemed to have
deserted his brain for the moment.

"*You're* the police chief?"

"Yes, ma'am," he said, automatically reaching
for his wallet badge. "Ethan Parker. Are you all
right?"

"Yes, but thank goodness you're here," she said,
her voice soft and throaty. Kind of sexy...except
he shouldn't be thinking about that when she was
obviously upset.

"Did you see who was outside?"

"Yes, ma'am," he answered, trying not to let his
gaze roam over her thinly dressed figure, shapely
legs and bare feet any more than absolutely necessary for police business. "They were raccoons—

two, to be precise—and I can assure you they were as frightened of me as you were of them.''

She sagged against the door frame, her breath fast and shallow. ''I feel so foolish. I thought maybe some kids were hanging around, or maybe vagrants. I really don't know anyone in this area, so I assumed whoever was making the noise wasn't friendly.''

''It's all right. I understand.''

She released her robe long enough to rake her fingers through dark blond, shoulder-length strands. Her other hand maintained a white-knuckled grip on the door frame. ''Are raccoons dangerous?''

''Not unless they're rabid.''

''Rabid!''

She looked absolutely shocked. She must be from the city if she was unfamiliar with one of the most common animals in Texas. And surely she'd heard of rabies. Or maybe that was the problem. Some people had an unreasonable fear of wild animals and the diseases they might carry.

''You shouldn't have to worry—'' The static signaling a call from the dispatcher was immediately followed by a request for his status.

The woman in the doorway jumped as though she'd taken a .45 to the chest.

Ethan cursed beneath his breath as he touched the communication unit attached to his uniform near his shoulder. ''Parker to dispatch,'' he answered more curtly than usual. ''Everything's fine out here, Ben. Just a few curious raccoons.''

His attention didn't waver from the woman as the dispatcher signed off. He wanted to reach out and comfort her, warm her hands between his larger ones, erase the look of panic from her wide brown eyes. Her palpable fear ate at his soul like acid.

"Would you like me to show you what made so much racket?" he asked gently.

"They're still here?" She peered into the darkness as if she could see around the house. Her hands now clutched the thin peach-colored robe as desperately as they'd gripped the door frame.

"No, although they might be up that tree over there—" he pointed "—watching us talk about them. There's a stack of trash they found mighty interesting. They were probably checking out the moving boxes to see if you'd left anything for them to eat." He smiled, but she didn't seem the least bit at ease with his good-ol'-boy routine. He decided another tactic was in order.

"You mentioned several possible intruders. Have you had any problems? This house was vacant for over a month."

She focused on him immediately, her eyes even wider, her shoulders rigid. She took a deep breath. "No, not really. I was just letting my imagination run wild. There's absolutely no reason anyone would know I'm here."

He frowned. "No family?"

"Of course, I have family," she said cautiously. "Just not here. And I haven't told them where I'm staying...yet." She shrugged dismissively, then tried a weak, unconvincing smile. "No big mystery."

He hadn't lost his instincts for investigation when he'd moved from Dallas to a quiet, small town. Miss Robin Cummings was running away from something—or someone. He'd bet his badge she wasn't about to let her family know where she was until she was good and ready.

"Are you in some kind of trouble, Miss Cummings?" he asked calmly, stepping closer. He needed to understand her fear. As an officer of the law, he told himself. Not as a man reacting to a woman who brought out every protective tendency he possessed.

"What do you mean? Why are you asking me that?"

"Because that's my job."

"I'm not in any trouble," she claimed, then paused. Her expression revealed what might be regret. "Unless you count an angry ex-fiancé and two parents who spent a fortune on a wedding that almost went off without a hitch."

Dammit, he did *not* need this complication in his life. Especially this particular problem. How was he, of all people, supposed to be rational, objective and sympathetic toward a woman who had left her angry, frustrated fiancé at the altar?

But then her lower lip started trembling, and she whispered, "It was going to be a very elegant wedding." She started shaking.

With another muttered curse, Ethan ignored his

own prejudice and years of training. He ignored the little voice in his head that told him this was a very stupid move, as he pulled her into his arms.

ROBIN WASN'T SURE how she ended up in the police chief's arms. She didn't know if comforting overly emotional women was standard police procedure. All she felt was the overwhelming relief of being wrapped snugly against a hard, male chest, with his strong hands soothing on her back, his heartbeat steady against her cheek.

She shouldn't crave the feeling. She definitely shouldn't get used to the comfort. And yet her arms clung to him, and her fingers pressed into the muscles of his back as she breathed in the scent of clean male and fresh starch. She sighed and closed her eyes, unable to resist the security this man—this stranger—represented.

There was nothing personal in his embrace…or in her reaction to him, she told herself as her tears and sniffles stopped. He was simply…tranquillity. Understanding. Acceptance in an unforgiving world. And he hadn't asked her about the foolish remarks she'd made. Her relief over the reprieve of not having to explain why she'd called off her wedding would have been enough to send her into his strong arms.

She could have stayed there for an eternity. Perhaps she did. Time ceased to exist as his hand stroked her upper back. Gradually, her breathing returned to normal. But then she realized his heartbeat was no longer steady and slow. And his chest wasn't the only hard, male part of him pressed tightly against her thin robe and skimpy cotton sleep shirt.

He must have felt the same awareness, because his hand stilled and he tensed. Robin pulled away at the same time as he cleared his throat and focused on the seemingly fascinating architectural details of the porch posts.

"I'm sorry for acting like such a...wuss," she said softly.

His smile appeared a bit strained as he looked back at her. He was embarrassed, she realized. Of her actions or his body's reaction?

"A wuss?" he asked. "You were afraid."

"Of raccoons."

His smile faded. "And you were upset."

She hugged her arms. Sooner or later, she was going to have to explore her feelings about the marriage that *didn't* go off without a hitch, but not now. Not yet. "Whatever. You showed me there's nothing to be afraid of." *If* she didn't count her response to the handsome police chief.

"I didn't say that. There's plenty to be cautious of out here. A lot of animals can be dangerous if they're hungry enough. But we hardly ever get a case of rabies."

She rubbed her arms against a sudden chill at the thought of salivating, fanged beasts. "I've never lived in the country before."

He glanced quickly at his watch, letting out a

long sigh. His expression told her he was battling some inner struggle. He was probably weighing common courtesy against correct procedure, counting the moments until he could escape from the crazy city woman.

"Parker to Dispatch," he said into the device pinned near his shoulder. His *wide, strong* shoulders. "Ten forty-two."

The dispatcher replied, but Robin couldn't hear what they said. She was just about to ask what the code meant when Chief Parker spoke.

"You're cold," he observed almost casually. "Would you like to go inside, Miss Cummings?"

"Well…"

"I'd be glad to give you a rundown on what you're likely to see out here. Kind of a *Country Primer*," he added with a reluctant smile that was way too sexy for a late-night official visit.

She hoped his observation about her being cold was based on her rubbing her arms and not the fact her thin robe was revealing more than she'd like him to see. The idea of his noticing her breasts caused a reaction that she hid by folding her arms across her chest. The friction was almost painful.

When she spoke, her voice sounded husky. Breathy. Sexy. Not at all like an interior decorator standing on a front porch in the middle of the night, wearing no makeup—and not much else, for that matter. "I don't want to keep you from your other duties."

"You're not. I'm off duty now. And like I said,

it's usually real quiet around here. This is the most excitement—"

His sudden pause was followed by what Robin strongly suspected was a blush from the local law enforcement officer, although she couldn't tell, since his back was to the porch light. The thought that she'd been the cause of so much "excitement" made her smile—to herself. No sense making him any more embarrassed than he already was.

On the other hand, she couldn't let him go so quickly. Not when the air was practically sparking with something very foreign and enticing. Maybe she was just relieved that there hadn't been a real threat to her security tonight. Maybe she wanted to focus on something besides her former fiancé and irate parents. Whatever the reason, she'd like the police chief's company for a while longer.

"I'll take you up on your offer. Why don't I fix us some coffee?"

He seemed genuinely surprised by her response. "You don't have to do that. You've had a scare."

"Which I'm now over, thanks to you." She reached for the storm door. "Please, come in for coffee and tell me all about these wild predators. I'd like to know how to tell a deranged killer from a hungry raccoon."

He smiled in an endearing, aw-shucks-ma'am manner that made her want to hug him tightly and tell him he was way too good to be true. Way too good-looking, too.

"If you're sure it's no trouble."

"I'd appreciate the company. Something tells me I won't be able to get to sleep anytime soon."

Especially if I keep thinking about Police Chief Ethan Parker, Robin silently added as she walked barefoot down the hallway to the "mother-in-law's room" she'd claimed as hers while staying at the Franklin house. Many of her clients in the suburbs had these bed and bath combinations separated from the other bedrooms. "Make yourself comfortable. I'll be right back."

She needed something more substantial to wear. There was no way she'd be able to continue a conversation—even one based on the flora and fauna of the Texas Hill Country—in this robe. Not when the chief looked so darn good in his crisp uniform and sexy, reluctant smile.

Robin paused, her smile fading as she pulled a T-shirt on over a sports bra and donned a pair of running shorts. She hadn't looked at the chief's hands. She hadn't noticed if he was wearing a wedding band. He might be married. There might be a Mrs. Parker waiting for her husband to come home.

He didn't *seem* in any hurry to get home to the missus. When Robin strolled into the kitchen a few minutes later, he was making coffee as if he owned the place. The distinctive aroma filled the room as the sputtering, hissing water filtered through the grounds.

"Find everything you need?" she asked, making more noise than necessary as she removed two mugs from the cabinet. Favorite mugs she'd placed there just hours before, as she'd unpacked the necessities she'd brought with her from her Houston condo.

"I hope you don't mind. I found some decaf. I didn't think you needed caffeine after what you've been through tonight."

"Decaf's fine. But like I said earlier, I don't want to keep you. Your…family might be expecting you home."

He turned his head to the side and smiled in a knowing way. "Is that the polite way to ask if I'm married?"

Robin stood straight, surprised she was so transparent. She really was rusty at this man-woman thing. Dating one man for two years would do that to a person. "I—"

"That's okay. You probably *should* have questions. Believe me, I don't usually… Well, let's just say that I haven't needed to comfort an upset woman in a long, long time."

"Is that your way of saying that you were just doing your job?" She placed the mugs on the counter next to the coffeemaker, then rested her hands on her hips. For some reason she didn't want to explore, she felt extraordinarily irritated by his remark.

"No, that's not what I meant." He rotated his neck, then ran a hand through his short, dark brown hair. His sheepish smile was totally different from the falsely charming one he'd given her on the porch, when he'd tried to convince her that strange noises in the night were nothing to worry about. "Look, I've never hugged a 9-1-1 caller before."

"Oh." She let her hands fall to her sides and concentrated on not smiling with feminine confidence. Perhaps she was still giddy with relief, but her reaction to Chief Parker was as out of character for her as he claimed his earlier behavior was for him. In a tiny corner of her mind, she knew being attracted to a man so quickly after her botched near-wedding was not smart, but for the moment she chose to ignore the warning.

Chapter Two

"I'm flattered I was your first 9-1-1 hug, then," she replied as casually as possible. "And to put my thinly veiled question another way, I hope your *wife* doesn't mind that you go around comforting hysterical women in the middle of the night."

Parker laughed. "I don't have a wife. Never have had one, although I have been close a time or two."

"Really? There's a story there, I'm sure, but I'm not bold enough to ask."

"Good, because I wouldn't answer. At least, not over a first cup of coffee when we're supposed to be talking about getting you acclimated to country living."

"Oh, yes. I almost forgot." She probably shouldn't have admitted that, she realized as she turned around and poured the coffee. Pasting a confident smile on her face, she walked the few steps to the table and placed the cup before him. "Cream or sugar?"

"No, thank you. I've learned to drink it black."

"You obviously have a tougher stomach than I

do,'' she said as she helped herself to sweetener and powdered creamer. Thank goodness she'd remembered to pack the basics, since the grocery in Ranger Springs had closed before she'd had a chance to go shopping.

''It's a prerequisite for law enforcement work.''

''I thought the dietary requirements included the ability to consume endless doughnuts.'' She took a sip of coffee, hoping he didn't take offense over her attempt at cop humor.

''Enough with the clichés,'' he said with a short chuckle. ''We have to stay a bit more healthy than a steady diet of doughnuts would allow.''

And he certainly did look healthy…and fit. She squirmed a bit in her seat, deciding she'd better change the subject quickly. ''So, what animals should I expect?''

He gave her a speculative look, but didn't pursue the personal remarks. Leaning back in his chair, he took a tentative sip of the hot coffee. ''The common ones are squirrels, raccoons, opossums, rabbits and deer. You'll probably have some foxes and coyotes visit, too, but you may never see them. They're pretty shy of humans. We've even had some cougars sighted, so be careful if you're out at night.''

''Cougars?'' She barely suppressed a shudder. ''I didn't realize I was *that* far out in the wild.''

''Actually, we keep intruding into their territory. San Antonio has spread pretty far north, and Austin is spreading south and west. We've built new roads and vacation homes through the Hill Country. The animals migrate where they can find food, which is often around humans.''

"I'll make sure they're not finding it at my back door.''

"That's the best thing you can do. Of course, the deer will eat anything in the yard—grass, trees, shrubs, flowers. It's hard to discourage them. The feed store has a few solutions, but a hungry deer is more persistent than anything I've seen so far.''

"I didn't know house-sitting was going to be so challenging,'' she said, shaking her head.

"You'll get used to it.'' He looked at her over the rim of his mug, his expression unreadable. The unspoken part of his remark echoed between them—*if you're going to be here that long.*

She didn't know the answer to that question.

"I'll try my best, especially the part about staying away from the meat-eaters.''

Parker leaned forward. "Don't make the mistake of treating any of the wild animals like house pets. Opossums have more teeth than any mammal in North America, and even a squirrel can seriously injure you by biting your finger instead of whatever you're trying to feed it. What appears cute and cuddly can quickly become dangerous.''

She wondered if his warning applied to off-duty police chiefs. "Don't worry. I'll limit my feeding to putting out seed for some nice, safe birds.''

"You'd be better off not putting anything out at all.''

"I like birds. I never get to feed them from my condo balcony."

"Then you'll also get squirrels and the rest. They like seed, too."

"You're not exactly a walking, talking advertisement for rural life, you know," she complained halfheartedly, unable to suppress a smile.

Parker chuckled. "No, I suppose I'm not. As a police officer, I tend to focus on prevention. If I can't prevent, I apprehend."

"And answer calls from hysterical women with a raccoon problem."

"That," he said, placing his empty mug on the table, "was a very rare event. I doubt I'll need to modify my job description, unless you're planning on calling in regularly."

She traced a cross over her heart. "I promise I'll look for four-legged visitors first."

He looked at her speculatively. "Will you?"

"Of course."

His expression grew more serious, more inquisitive, reminding Robin that he was, as a law enforcement officer, a trained interrogator. "You were pretty upset—maybe not a hundred percent from the raccoons."

She shrugged, not wanting to discuss the subject. She wasn't sure why she'd brought it up. "Newhouse jitters. A change in life-style. I'm fine now."

He didn't look convinced, but, thankfully, didn't argue. Instead, he pushed back his chair and rose, towering over her until she was forced to stand, or get a crick in her neck.

"I'd better let you get some sleep. Are you sure you're okay?"

"I'm fine. And I really enjoyed the coffee, and the conversation."

"I'll have the next patrol officer drive by a few times tonight, just to make sure you're safe."

"I'm sure that's unnecessary."

"I'll sleep better knowing you're okay."

"I...I suppose that's a good idea." She smiled. "I wouldn't want to be surrounded by angry raccoons."

"Or held hostage by hungry deer," he teased.

"No." Her smile faded as the joking ended. She felt the tension building now just as surely as she'd smelled coffee brewing earlier.

"Well, then, thank you for the coffee," he said.

He seemed to take up way too much space in the kitchen. His blue eyes, as warm and dark as the coffee he'd brewed, looked at her in a very un-policeman-like manner.

"You're welcome," she answered, her voice an octave lower than when she'd stood on her front porch in her sleep shirt and robe. "Thanks for fixing it." Darn it, she'd already thanked him for that once. Did he think she was babbling? Well, perhaps she was.

"No problem."

The silence stretched on for just a moment too long. A breathless, quiet moment that made her forget about everything but the man standing before her. But then he shifted his weight, his hand automatically resting on a holster that held a large and dangerous-looking pistol, and she remembered that he was a law enforcement officer, and that she was a new resident who'd called in with an emergency.

Perhaps he was just being friendly. Maybe she was imagining this tension between them. *Or you could just be mentally exhausted and rambling,* she told herself as she gripped the back of her chair.

"Thank you for coming out, Chief Parker."

"You're welcome. And the name's Ethan."

"Ethan." A strong name. A simple, basic name—one without nicknames and unusual spellings.

He smiled at her again, then picked up his flashlight and walked toward the front door. She followed behind, a sense of *déjà vu* reminding her she'd walked guys to the door before. Dates…and one nice, safe fiancé. Not police chiefs she barely knew.

"By the way," he said, pausing as he pushed open the front door, "I did come out because you called. That was duty. I stayed because I wanted to. Sitting down and sharing a cup of coffee had nothing to do with my professional responsibilities."

She looked up at his well-defined features and Mel-Gibson-blue eyes. Her heart beat so fast, she wondered if he could see the blood rushing through her veins. "Thank you for telling me."

"I just wanted you to understand the difference.

I don't come on to women I meet in the line of duty.''

"No hugging?" she whispered.

"No." His eyes focused solely on her lips. She couldn't help herself; she licked away the dryness in a nervous gesture.

"No kissing, either." He leaned forward ever so slightly. The night noises sounded overly loud, drowning out her heartbeat as she lost herself in his eyes. But then he blinked, startling both himself and her. He jerked upright, the moment gone as quickly as a cricket's chirp.

He started to say something, just as the dispatcher's voice came over the communication unit. "Dispatch to Parker. What's your 40?"

He punched a small button. "Leaving the Franklin house right now."

"You had a call. Someone checking up on you." Even a couple of feet away from the communication device, Robin heard the humor in the dispatcher's voice.

Ethan smiled. "Tell her I'm on my way."

Her? He'd said he didn't have a wife. Then who was checking up on him this late at night?

Robin frowned, envisioning an impatient girlfriend waiting for the police chief, but apparently he didn't pick up on her...unease. She refused to call the feeling anything else.

He seemed in a sudden hurry to be anywhere but her front porch. "I'll see you soon," he said, backing through the doorway. "Keep yourself safe."

"I will." She tried not to frown.

"Good night, Robin."

"Good night."

She reached for the storm door, securing it as he strode toward the patrol car. Then she folded her arms and leaned against the door facing, her jumbled impressions of the last call colliding with images of Ethan, the man, and Chief Parker, the protector. And all of it churned by exhaustion that left her longing for a thick, soft mattress and twelve hours of uninterrupted sleep.

A few seconds later, he started the engine of the patrol car, then turned on his headlights. As she slowly closed the heavy wood door, he pulled out of the driveway onto the county road, scattering a few errant leaves and some small puffs of dirt on his way back to town.

Leaving her with more questions than answers.

THE NEXT MORNING, Ethan headed to the Four Square Café for his lunch break. He needed a simple answer: who was Robin Cummings? Why did a born-and-bred city girl move to a small town, even temporarily? His instincts told him she was the type of person who was close to her family. Who had friends who'd comfort her during an obviously trying time. She'd said her wedding was to be an expensive one, which meant money. So if she needed to get away, why had she chosen Ranger Springs, of all places?

As he pushed open the country-style door, the

jingling bell announced his arrival. The smells of chicken-fried steak, French fries and sizzling bacon drifted through the high service window at the back of the restaurant. Conversations, which had been humming along as he'd entered, subsided, replaced by the *clink* of knives and forks placed on Texas Places of Interest paper place mats. Heads turned in his direction.

Eating lunch in a public place wasn't really news, but as he looked into the curious faces of the diners, he half expected a headline to that effect in the *Springs Gazette's* Sunday edition. Perhaps he had been going home for lunch fairly often, or eating one of Aunt Bess's meatloaf sandwiches at his desk, but surely he hadn't become so much of a curiosity. Surely, he hadn't become that predictable. *Boring,* some might say, he thought with a frown.

"How are you, Thelma?" he asked the newspaper editor as he walked past her table. She was having lunch with the perpetually strawberry-blond owner of the town's only beauty shop. "Good afternoon, Joyce."

Both women acknowledged his greeting, but he didn't pause and chat. Not when the object of his search was seated in the last red vinyl booth, picking her way through a Cobb salad, her red hair sleeked back in a no-nonsense style that matched her conservative pale yellow dress. At one time, the matchmakers in town had tried to push him toward the career-minded real estate agent. His experience with women who valued their careers more than their relationships had made him understandably shy of getting involved with her.

He passed by Jimmy Mack Branson, Ranger Springs's hardware expert, who was eating lunch with Pastor Carl Schleipinger and banker Ralph Biggerstaff. Nodding at the men, he continued to the rear of the café.

"Afternoon, Gina Mae," he said, creasing his hat to keep his hands busy. He didn't want the crafty real estate lady to know he was just a tad nervous about approaching her.

"Chief Parker! How are you?"

"Fine. Do you have a minute?"

"Of course. Have a seat." She gathered up some papers she'd spread across the table's gray Formica surface. "I was just working on a new listing. You're not interested in a larger house, are you?"

"No, I'm real happy where I am."

"Well, then, what can I do for you?"

"I drove out to the Franklin house last night. I suppose you rented it out."

"Actually, the Franklins wanted a house-sitter. I thought you knew that."

So Robin had told the truth to the dispatcher last night. "I know they're out of the country for another two or three months. I wanted to make sure the person living there was legit."

"They weren't looking for rent—just someone to care for the place and the plants while they're gone. You know how dangerous it is to leave a house vacant."

"Absolutely. Anyway," he said, getting the conversation back on track, "I met the new occupant. She'd been startled by some raccoons." *And upset about the wedding that hadn't taken place to the fiancé she'd stood up at the altar.* Not that he had any intention of asking Gina Mae about that particular detail. He just wanted to know more about the town's newest resident. *The one who looked really great, even late at night, and could laugh at herself with refreshing honesty.*

"Ah, yes," Gina Mae said, her sudden interest in the conversation making her push the half-eaten salad aside. "A very nice young woman from Houston. An interior decorator, I believe."

He could hear the unspoken comment: a nice *single* young woman. "Miss Cummings," he added, keeping his comments professional.

"That's right. But you probably knew that before you went out to the house, didn't you?"

Ethan frowned. "What do you mean?"

"Your aunt. That's how I met Robin."

"My aunt knows Miss Cummings?"

"You didn't know? Well, yes. At least, she knows Robin Cummings's great-aunt. They're old friends."

"Really," Ethan said, his mind spinning with questions. Why hadn't Aunt Bess mentioned her friend's great-niece? Why had she arranged for Robin to move to Ranger Springs without letting him know?

"I hope I didn't say anything wrong," Gina Mae

said, a frown creasing her smooth forehead. "Your aunt didn't say any of this was a secret."

"No, I'm sure it's not. She probably just forgot to mention the connection."

"Probably."

Ethan stared at the faux marble Formica, wondering if Aunt Bess's forgetfulness was deliberate or accidental. Maybe he should take off his police "hat" and start thinking like a nephew. Aunt Bess wasn't getting any younger. Not only did she keep house for him, but she prepared several hearty meals a week. He'd told her time and again that she didn't need to work so hard, that he could afford to hire help, but she'd insisted she enjoyed taking care of him and the house. She'd said she liked staying active and useful, especially since her husband's death four years ago.

"Chief Parker?"

He mentally shook himself out of his musings. "Sorry, Gina Mae. I was just thinking about Aunt Bess." He eased out of the booth, then retrieved his hat. "I hope I didn't disturb your lunch."

"No, not at all. You tell Bess hello for me, you hear?"

"I'll do that. Have a good day."

He walked out of the restaurant, ignoring more speculative looks that the townspeople might give him. He was sure Thelma and Joyce would find a reason to stop by Gina Mae's booth after they finished their lunch, and that the men would try their best to overhear the conversation.

Okay by him. He hadn't said anything that any of them could turn into gossip. After all, he hadn't mentioned that he'd held Robin Cummings in his arms last night. Or stared at her bare legs and firmly rounded breasts. Or sat up late sipping coffee while they discussed wildlife.

Not his "wild life." By anyone's standards, his life-style was as tame as that of a baby animal at a petting zoo—without the petting. Again, that dreaded word—*boring*—insinuated itself into his mind. He pushed the thought aside.

Ethan jammed his hat on his head and walked back to his office at the municipal building. He could certainly recognize a mystery when presented with the evidence. And his own aunt held the clue.

As ROBIN PULLED into the parking lot of a fast food restaurant on the outskirts of Ranger Springs, she was driving one of the only sporty coupes in an asphalt sea where pickup trucks and aging sedans rested like modest boats moored in a marina. Her heart skipped a beat when she spotted a police car in the first row, but she told herself that didn't mean Ethan Parker was inside. One of his officers was probably taking a supper break.

While she waited in line, Robin looked around the seating area. Since she didn't know anyone else in town yet, she searched for someone in a law enforcement uniform. *Just out of curiosity,* she told herself. She didn't really expect to find the police chief having supper. But her eyes settled on the dark hair of a man with wide shoulders and perfect posture. His back was to her, and he was seated, not with a gorgeous girlfriend, but with an elderly lady who reminded her of her own great-aunt Sylvia.

"Miss? May I take your order?"

Now she jerked her attention back to the counter, where a perky blonde in bright polyester waited.

She placed her order, her glance returning to the man she thought might be Ethan Parker. He was dressed in street clothes, so she couldn't tell without getting a glimpse of his profile.

Suddenly, the older lady caught her gaze, giving her a friendly little smile. Embarrassed, Robin smiled back automatically, then turned her attention to the plastic tray that awaited her burger and shake. She really shouldn't ogle the locals. The man probably wasn't Ethan Parker, anyway.

Except, how many guys in Ranger Springs could look anywhere near as good as the compassionate police chief?

A sense of traveling back in time rippled through her as she took her tray and proceeded back to the molded vinyl seats and booths. She half expected Crissy Caldwell, her best friend from high school, to scoot up beside her and ask if she'd seen that really gorgeous new hunk in chemistry class. Only this time, Robin was the "new kid in school," and she was bound and determined not to blush when she deliberately walked by the broad-shouldered man with his white-haired companion.

Again, the older lady smiled at her. Robin slowed to get a good look at the man sitting across from the friendly woman.

"Are you, by any chance, Sylvia Murphy's great-niece?" the lady asked.

Robin stopped abruptly. "Yes, I am. Robin Cummings." Awareness hit, and Robin smiled with sincerity. "Don't tell me you're Bess Delgado!"

"Yes!" The older woman looked delighted. "I thought that was you from Sylvia's description. She hasn't sent a picture since you were a young teenager."

"I suppose I have changed in fifteen years." Robin laughed, her attention suddenly focused on the man trying to maneuver out of the booth to stand. "Please, don't get up," she said as her eyes traveled up the length of his jeans-clad legs, subtly plaid shirt and broad shoulders. Up to his handsome face and intense blue eyes.

She tried to keep the surprise out of her expression, but her voice sounded breathless when she said, "Police Chief Parker!"

"Hello, Miss Cummings," he greeted her. Polite, but warm, she thought. Or maybe the warmth was coming from her. She felt her heart rate increase as the blood raced through her. Definitely high school days. She hadn't felt this kind of excitement since the boy she'd had a crush on for years had asked her to Homecoming. She certainly hadn't felt it for her fiancé.

Chapter Three

"Join us," Bess requested in a tone of voice reserved for gracious-but-demanding older ladies. "I know you've met my nephew. Ethan was just scolding me for not telling him you'd moved to town."

Robin placed her tray on the table, wondering on which side she should sit. Bess didn't move, so Robin looked at Ethan. His broad shoulders took up most of the molded vinyl seat. With a slight smile, he politely slid over to make room.

"Really?" she answered. Why in the world would he expect his aunt to tell him about her?

"Now, Aunt Bess, I didn't scold you. I was just surprised that you arranged for Miss Cummings to move to town, since you hadn't mentioned your involvement."

"Well, I can't remember everything, can I?" she answered with a laugh. "I'm just glad there was a place available when Sylvia called. I knew our little town was just what you needed to…well, you know."

"Um, yes." Robin took a deep breath. A stab of

guilt over her actions spoiled her appetite. Could she ever really live down walking out on her fiancé? She wasn't sure, but she certainly didn't want to discuss her personal life in this crowded restaurant. She smiled in her most convincing manner. "I'm sure I'll be very happy here for a while."

"Of course you will," Bess said.

Of course I will. She just needed a little time. A little distraction. And at the moment, she couldn't think of anything more distracting than the man sitting beside her. The man who'd held her in his arms last night.

Bess Delgado must be the woman who had called Ethan's dispatcher to check up on him last night, Robin realized. The woman she'd thought was a girlfriend…or more. The thought of the sexy chief of police living with his doting aunt brought a secret smile to Robin's face.

"My great-aunt Sylvia is going strong. She's busy with the charity flower show right now."

"Sylvia always did have a green thumb," Bess said with a fond smile. "We met at the Tyler Rose Festival, back in the early fifties. We've been friends ever since, finding we had far more in common than our love of growing things."

"Go ahead and eat your meal," Ethan offered. "We promise not to keep you from your burger."

Robin nodded, then automatically took a bite despite her waning appetite. Not filet mignon, but tasty. She refused to think about how many calories she was consuming, even though she no longer had to fit into a creamy-white designer wedding gown—with dozens of seed pearls and yards of lace, she reminded herself with a pang of longing. Not that she'd wanted to go through with the ceremony. But that dress had been her dream wedding gown, and she regretted having to store it for sometime in the future—sometime that might never come.

She felt self-conscious after a minute or so. Ethan and Bess had finished their meals and were taking sips of their beverages just to have something to do, Robin suspected. She placed her burger down and dabbed her mouth with the napkin. "I broke down the boxes and took the trash to the nearest Dumpster," she told Ethan. "Maybe the raccoons will leave me alone tonight."

"Oh, they'll probably come around looking for a meal, but if they don't find anything, they shouldn't make any racket."

"I wouldn't want to call 9-1-1 again," she teased, hoping to lighten her mood. "I'll get a reputation as a crazy city woman."

"Not as long as I back you up. I'll be glad to vouch for the presence of wild animals."

"But not dangerous ones," she replied before taking a sip of milk shake.

He smiled slightly, his gaze straying to her lips as they puckered around the straw. "You never know."

Robin felt a blush creeping up her neck. She hadn't blushed in years. Maybe she was reverting back to high school behavior. Maybe she was just really confused about all her feelings lately. She just hoped Bess hadn't noticed anything…strange in their banter. Robin didn't want to give one of her great-aunt's best friends the wrong idea.

Because she really wasn't interested in getting involved with anyone. Even someone as handsome and compelling as Ethan Parker. Even if he did make her pulse race. She wasn't going back to Gig, but eventually she'd return to her real life in Houston. To her business, friends and family. A short fling with a small-town lawman wasn't in her nature.

"Robin, you must come over and visit me tomorrow. I know you probably have better things to do than spend your day with an old lady, but I'd just adore the company."

"I'd love to visit," she said sincerely. "Just tell me when and where."

"I live with Ethan, you know. He needs someone to take care of him."

The police chief moaned. "Aunt Bess, you know I can get by on my own. You're living with me because we both want it that way. You're family."

"Of course, dear," Bess said in a tone that meant *I'm rolling my eyes at you.*

Robin stifled a chuckle. "Is there someplace we could go for lunch?"

Ethan took one of his cards from his wallet badge and wrote his home address on it for her. "And this is our home number," he said, looking up with his sparkling blue eyes, "just in case you need to report any midnight visitors and prefer to bypass the emergency operator.''

BESS WAITED UNTIL Ethan went outside to water the garden before she called Sylvia in Houston. Her longtime friend had a condo in the same building as Robin, and spent a lot of time with the girl. When Sylvia had called to say her great-niece had finally come to her senses and called off the wedding, Bess had heard the relief in her friend's voice. Sylvia obviously hadn't thought the match was a good one. And she thought Robin needed to get away for a while. Someplace nice and quiet, away from worrisome parents and upset, would-be in-laws. Not to mention the jilted fiancé.

Bess had cringed a bit at the knowledge that Robin's young man's hopes had been dashed. After all, she'd been through that before with… But that was another story, and she wanted to focus on Sylvia's great-niece. So she'd thought of the lovely Franklin house, sitting vacant on that wooded lot. What a wonderful place for Robin to recuperate from her wounded pride.

"Sylvia," Bess greeted her friend. "I met your lovely great-niece today." She proceeded to tell Sylvia about the chance meeting between Robin and Ethan at the hamburger place. "You should have seen the two of them tonight. The sparks fairly flew!"

"You don't say!"

"Yes, I do, and I'm all for it. Ethan has just

about given up on finding a wife, and I know Robin is understandably shy about getting involved again. That's why I think we need to give them a little push in the right direction.''

''What did you have in mind?''

''Well, I think I need a little vacation.''

''Really?''

''Yes. Ethan is already convinced I'm getting forgetful because I didn't tell him Robin was moving in. He thinks I work too hard. If I went to San Antonio to visit Grace and Margaret at the retirement home, then Ethan would need someone to come by his house and check on him. Maybe fix him a home-cooked meal. Watch a little television with him.''

''I'm not sure…''

''Oh, I know this will work. All I need to do is ask Robin to help me out by looking after Ethan for a short time. Then you can call Ethan and ask him to watch out for Robin while she's staying in town. You could suggest he take her to a movie, or out to dinner.''

''I thought you only had two restaurants and no movie theater.''

''We're not that far from Fredericksburg or Kerrville. What could be more romantic than a nice evening drive through the Hill Country?''

''You have a point.''

''Of course I do! Oh, Sylvia, I know I'm right about this. Those two would be perfect for each other, if they could just spend enough time together to realize it.''

''You may be right, and I'll be glad to go along. There's just one thing you should know.''

''What's that?''

''My dear, sweet Robin can't even microwave a frozen dinner without burning it to crisp.''

''AUNT BESS, I'M HOME,'' Ethan announced as he stepped from the late-afternoon heat into the air-conditioned kitchen.

Ethan's shift had been fairly chaotic for a normally quiet, midweek day in the summer. Some cattle escaped their fence and wandered onto the state highway, leading to a two-car accident. No one was seriously injured, but he and his deputy had spent most of the afternoon directing traffic away from the evasive beasts.

As he pulled into his driveway about a half-hour late for dinner, he hoped Aunt Bess hadn't fixed anything that might fall, congeal or generally taste terrible if it wasn't served exactly on time. She was rather proud of her cooking, and rightly so. He'd rather be trampled by a dozen stray cows than disappoint his favorite relative.

A dozen different smells filled the air, but he couldn't pinpoint what she'd prepared for dinner. The cabinet was lined with various plastic containers, each one neatly labeled in his aunt's precise handwriting.

"Ethan, I'm glad you're home," his aunt said briskly. "I've had such a hectic day."

"You and me, both." He walked to the normally cheerful, uncomplaining lady and kissed her cheek. "What's wrong?"

"Oh, just this and that. I spent some time thinking about what you said the other day, and I'm afraid you're right. Perhaps I do sometimes try to do too much."

"You're not feeling ill, are you? Did you fall, or—"

"No, no," Bess said, waving off his questions. "Not yet, anyway. I'm just not as young as I once was, and today I realized I need to take things a bit easier."

"I've been trying to tell you that, Aunt Bess." Ethan placed his arm around her shoulder, noticing how small she was. Of course, she'd always been tiny, but now she seemed even more frail. He steered her away from the kitchen and back into the living room. "Have you been to the doctor? You'd tell me if something was wrong, wouldn't you?"

"Of course I would, dear." She patted his hand as he urged her to sit on the sofa. "But I've decided I need a little vacation. I'm going to visit Margaret and Grace in San Antonio for a week or so. I'll leave tomorrow morning after you go to work. That way I'll get in to San Antonio after the morning rush."

"I'm sure you'll have a great time with your

friends. Just relax and don't worry about a thing here. I'll be fine.''

"I know you will, although I would feel better if I didn't think you'd spend every night alone, watching baseball and reruns. Or working extra hours.'' Bess sighed. ''At least you won't starve. I made some of your favorites—roast beef, meatballs and lasagna.''

His aunt didn't paint a very flattering picture of him, although he couldn't say it was totally inaccurate. He did enjoy an occasional baseball game in the evenings, and he had been known to go back to the office if he didn't have a lot to do at home. But he also met with citizen groups and spoke on public safety. He filled in as an umpire at Little League games when one of the regulars couldn't make it. And he worked out in the extra bedroom he'd set up with exercise equipment.

Ethan decided to deflect her fixation on his bachelor state, first by ignoring her comments, then by changing the subject. He'd learned more about evasive tactics in the last two years than he had during his FBI training.

His aunt pushed up from the couch and started toward the kitchen. ''There is one thing you could do for me while I'm gone.''

"Anything, Aunt Bess. You know that.''

"Take a little time for yourself. Ask a nice young lady out to a movie and dinner. Don't work all the time instead of sitting around the house.''

"Aunt Bess, this is a small town. The chief of

police doesn't need to be dating every single woman in the area.''

"How about just one single woman under the age of thirty-five?''

"There aren't that many.''

"I can think of a few,'' his aunt said in a knowing voice.

"I'm sure you can.'' And one of them was no doubt the great-niece of Bess's good friend in Houston. "I'm not looking for a relationship.''

"Then how about a little fun? It's not normal for a man your age to be so, well…so celibate.''

"Aunt Bess!''

"Well, it's not.'' She left him standing in the doorway, shaking his head as she hustled off to prepare dinner. Just before she placed a casserole in the microwave, she turned back to him with a twinkle in her eye. "I swear, Ethan, half the men in the retirement home get more action than you do.''

SINCE ROBIN HAD LONG AGO unpacked her two suitcases, she had plenty of time to explore the house and make an inventory of items she needed from the store. Unfortunately, her current bank balance wasn't nearly as healthy as her wish list. She'd have to economize while she was hiding out in Ranger Springs, but at least she had the satisfaction of knowing her bridesmaids had been reimbursed for their gowns and shoes.

Not that any of them had been hurting for money,

but she would have felt even more remorse over calling off the wedding if she'd left them with the bill for clothes they'd probably never use again. After all, most of them had half a dozen used bridesmaid dresses hanging in the closet, if they hadn't been donated to charity or taken to a consignment store. The difference between her and her friends was that her beautiful *un*used wedding gown now kept her bridesmaid dresses company.

She paused, her fingers clutching the pen and paper, as she imagined her friends and family wondering where she was, what she'd been thinking when she'd canceled the wedding just three weeks before she was to walk down the aisle with one of Houston's most eligible men. Everyone except Great-aunt Sylvia had accepted her engagement to Gig Harrelson as a given.

Robin wasn't sure what her aunt hadn't liked about Gig. He was a former football player—albeit second-string at Texas A&M—with the blond hair and handsome features one would expect from a true ''golden boy.'' He came from one of the best families, circulated easily in several different social circles, and could relate well to both men and women. Gig was an asset to his father's banking business and would have made a perfectly wonderful husband.

Maybe she didn't *want* a perfect husband, Robin mused. Maybe Gig had been a little too perfect, from his straight white teeth to his designer sportswear. Had her heart ever raced when he'd held her in his arms? Had she felt juvenile excitement at just a glimpse of him across a crowded restaurant?

Maybe getting away to this small town, to a totally different environment, had been the best idea. Not because she wanted a relationship with another man, but because she needed to put the last one in perspective.

Shaking her head, Robin returned to her inventory, but was interrupted again when the phone rang.

"Hello?" she answered.

"Robin, dear, I'm so glad you're home. I have a favor to ask."

Since the days were stretching ahead of her like a blank slate, a favor for Bess Delgado sounded pretty good. "What can I do for you?"

"I'm taking a little vacation to San Antonio to visit some friends. Ethan is going to be home, though, and I just hate the thought of him all alone."

Robin took the cordless phone and started pacing the living room. Oh, no. Surely Bess didn't expect a stranger to keep her nephew company! Robin sure didn't want to give the man the wrong idea by spending personal time with him.

"Robin?"

"Yes, I'm here."

"I know you're just in town for a short time, but I feel as though I've known you for most of your life. Your Great-aunt Sylvia was always telling me about your latest triumphs and tribulations. That's why I'd like you to spend some time with Ethan. Like most bachelors, he'll probably spend hours sitting in front of the television unless he has something to do.''

She should tell Bess ''no.'' All she had to do was think of some really good excuse, something that rang true, yet would let her great-aunt's sweet friend down lightly.

Instead, she heard herself say, ''What did you have in mind?''

''Oh, nothing major, dear. Just sharing a meal. You might suggest he take you around to see some of the sights. There's a very scenic drive near Wimberley.''

Robin paused at the side window, looking out at the pecan trees and remembering the late-night ruckus that had brought Ethan to her house that first night. Recalling the way he'd held her so firmly and listened so compassionately to her explanation of everything from growing up in the city to running away from her wedding. ''Bess, I'm not sure that's a good idea. I'm sure Ethan has other things to do.''

''Oh, he works hard, but most of his friends around here are married couples, and busy with their own lives in the evenings. And he's not dating anyone, so that wouldn't be a problem.''

Robin scrambled for another excuse, this one closer to the real reason she needed to decline. ''He might get the wrong idea.''

''You just tell him you're new in town and you'd

like a little company. I can't imagine him turning you down."

"I don't want him to think I'm imposing on him." *Or worse yet, asking him out on a date.*

"He won't, dear. Ethan's very nice. If he's told me once, he's told me a dozen times that he's not looking for a steady girl."

A steady girl. Robin had to smile as she strolled across the room. Had she ever heard that expression used? Probably when she'd been flipping through the old-movie channel and caught one of those Doris Day films from the fifties.

"I'd have such a better time with my friends if I knew Ethan wasn't sitting home alone every night."

Bess really knew how to pour on the guilt, Robin silently acknowledged. She sighed as she picked up a very good reproduction porcelain St. Charles spaniel on the mantel, then said, "I suppose I could give him a call, just to be friendly. I'm not so sure about suggesting anything as time-consuming as a drive through the country."

"Whatever you're comfortable with, dear." Bess paused, giving Robin the impression the older lady was weighing her next words. "Perhaps the two of you could share a meal at Ethan's house. I've fixed a variety of food. It's all in the freezer."

That sounded simple enough, but again, Robin wasn't entirely comfortable with asking herself into Ethan's personal world. Going to his house and rummaging through his freezer seemed so…intimate. Interacting with him in his professional capacity, or even seeing him in public was a different matter.

''I'll think about it, Bess. That's all I can promise. I just don't want him to feel uncomfortable.''

''I'm sure Ethan will be glad to hear from you. I just know he'll get lonely while I'm gone,'' Bess added with a sigh.

Robin wondered if she'd have the nerve to pick up the phone and give the good-looking police chief a nice, friendly call. For the second time that week, she felt as though she'd slipped back into high school. Only this time, a member of the older generation was encouraging her to ask a boy out for a date instead of telling her that good girls simply didn't *do* that sort of thing.

Robin placed the white-and-brown china dog back on the mantel. Oh, for the good old days.

Chapter Four

Ethan had almost banished Robin Cummings from his mind the day after his aunt left for San Antonio, basically because he'd been busy meeting with the Fourth of July planning committee. Since several streets had to be blocked and traffic stopped on Main Street, his officers were crucial to a successful parade. But as soon as he'd pulled into his drive and cut the engine of his Bronco the following evening, his thoughts returned to the woman he'd already sworn he'd never date.

He hadn't had a chance when Sylvia had called him from Houston. She'd wanted to talk to Bess, but seemed more than happy to chat with him, instead. And then she'd pulled out the big guns—her fear that her poor, lonely great-niece would languish in the big family home where she was housesitting, so far from Houston. Hundreds of miles from her friends and family. All alone, with only memories to keep her company....

He would have seemed a total cad if he'd said ''no'' to the very nice lady who was one of Bess's best friends. He would have seemed petty if he'd come up with an excuse why he couldn't possibly share a friendly evening meal with an attractive, single woman. A friend of the family. In the end, he couldn't avoid a promise to Sylvia that he'd ask her niece out on a "neighborly" date.

After all, he couldn't have the citizens of Ranger Springs—even the temporary ones—languishing from loneliness, he thought with a chuckle and a shake of his head.

So now he stood in front of the white wall phone in the kitchen, Robin's number at the Franklin home written on a grocery receipt, his mouth as dry as the Texas prairie in August.

"I promised," he reminded himself, his voice rusty. What he needed was an icy-cold longneck to help him through this, but even if he used the excuse of a dry throat, drinking didn't seem right. He didn't want his brain to be fuddled by alcohol when he called Robin.

With no excuses left, he picked up the phone and dialed her number.

"POLICE CHIEF PARKER?" Had Robin's thoughts of him conjured up the call? All afternoon she'd been debating how to approach him, and now he'd landed in her lap, so to speak.

"Please, call me Ethan."

Even better. So this wasn't an official call. "How are you, Ethan?"

"Fine." He seemed to be moving around. She

heard footsteps, then the rustle of paper. "My aunt's out of town."

Should she admit she knew? Somehow, telling Ethan about Bess's phone call and request seemed disloyal to the older lady. So Robin settled on the very neutral "Really?"

"Yes, she's gone to San Antonio for a few days to visit friends." Another pause, this one silent. "I was wondering how you were doing. Settling in okay?"

"I'm fine. No more scary critters," she said with a chuckle. She settled on the arm of the taupe-and-cream damask sofa, wondering if he knew why he'd called...or if he planned to let her in on the secret.

"Good." He was moving around again. She heard the *pop* of a cap, then the sound of him drinking. She didn't know what beverage he was consuming, but she could almost see the strong column of his neck as he swallowed. The image made her own throat go dry.

"I'm not exactly a brilliant conversationalist, am I," he said with humor in his voice.

"I'm not doing a great job, either, and I usually spend a lot of time on the phone."

"In your job?"

"Yes. Talking to clients and suppliers. Setting up appointments and checking inventories. Sometimes I call all over Texas, trying to track down one particular piece I've seen at a show or at a vendor's booth."

"You're not working now, are you?"

"No, not while I'm staying in Ranger Springs."
She missed her work, but she couldn't establish a
new clientele for only two months in a town the
size of this one. Besides, thinking about her life
back in Houston would only make her more vulnerable to a friendly voice and a fetching smile. She
needed to keep a clear mind about Bess's nephew,
no matter how much she enjoyed his attention.

After all, he might be lonely, as Bess had mentioned. His call might not be personal. She frowned
at the idea of being just another voice on the end
of the phone line.

"I suppose you have a lot of free time," he re-
marked.

His statement left a lot unsaid, but still caused
her pulse to accelerate. "Yes, too much, actually.
Since I've already toured the town and I can't redecorate the house I'm staying in, I'm at a loss for
things to do."

Another swallow. Another pause. "Would you
like to go to dinner?"

"Because you think I'm bored?" she asked cautiously. "Or do you ask all the newcomers in your
town to dinner?"

He fell silent, as if she'd surprised him. Perhaps
she had. She'd startled herself by abruptly asking
for honesty—but she'd rather watch summer reruns
than go on a pity date with a man as appealing as
Ethan Parker.

"No, because I'd like to take you to one of my

favorite places. And I thought you might like to see a little more of the Hill Country.''

"In that case, I'd love to go to dinner with you," she said as her heart rate hiked a little higher. And as she told herself again that she shouldn't think of it as going on an actual *date* with the police chief. "When?"

"Tomorrow night?"

"Great." And to pay him back for this date, which was probably part reluctant attraction, part neighborly duty, she could ask him over for a meal. Then Bess would be happy, and Robin wouldn't have to intrude in the other lady's kitchen—or in Ethan's house. After she'd fulfilled her responsibility to Ethan's aunt, she could make it clear that she wasn't going to get romantically involved with anyone right now—no matter how appealing and friendly he was.

She'd become so much more aware of responsibility lately, when she'd disappointed the wedding party and guests. But she had an obligation to the truth, too. Getting married for the wrong reasons was an even worse offense. Surely her family and friends would realize that soon. Perhaps many of them already did. Great-aunt Sylvia understood, or maybe she was simply relieved, since she hadn't been overjoyed even with the engagement.

In two months or so, Robin hoped she could return to her life without seeing disappointment on the faces of those she loved. And if they couldn't accept her decision to call off the wedding…well, perhaps they didn't love her as much as she thought.

So she'd keep her word to Bess, and she'd be honest with Ethan. She wasn't looking for a new life in a small town any more than he seemed to want a serious relationship.

ETHAN THOUGHT THE NIGHT had gone rather well. He'd successfully controlled his attraction to Robin all through the early evening drive on nearly deserted country highways. Robin had been delighted with the steep hills, winding roads, abundant trees and quaint stone houses; he'd been captivated by her enjoyment of the simple ride through the Hill Country. He'd resisted touching her hand, stroking her arm, or running his fingers through her silky blond hair whenever he glanced at her.

All through dinner, he'd been the perfect gentleman. He'd held out her chair, refusing to lean forward and nuzzle her neck when his libido urged him closer. He'd ignored the low light and candles on each table, and the glorious sunset they'd witnessed together through the multipaned windows. He'd laughed, listened and truly enjoyed the companionship during a delicious meal of German specialties at one of his favorite restaurants. They'd both been too full of the good, hearty food to stay for dessert, so there was nothing left to do but return, just after twilight, to Ranger Springs.

Robin was quiet during the thirty-minute drive, but whenever Ethan glanced at her, he noticed a slight smile on her face. Yes, the evening had gone well. He didn't believe she suspected how nervous he'd been about asking her out to dinner, nor did she know of his heightened awareness of her during the meal.

All in all, his Aunt Bess would be proud of him.

As he pulled the Bronco into the driveway of the Franklin home, the night surrounded them like a black glove. The porch lights Robin had turned on earlier seemed far away from the gravel drive where he'd parked. As soon as he turned off the engine, the silence of the night added to the sense of isolation. Not since he'd been a hormone-laden young man could he remember feeling such charged anticipation.

"I had a good time tonight, Ethan." Her voice sounded as soft as the velvet darkness outside.

He unbuckled his seat belt and turned toward her, thankful for the bucket seats that separated them. Otherwise, he'd be sorely tempted to pull her into his arms and claim that the night wasn't yet over.

But it was. He had to accept the fact that Robin Cummings was not for him. He wasn't about to let his physical attraction for her overrule his common sense. She was here only temporarily; he'd established a new life for himself in this small town. She belonged among the wealthy clients and excitement of the city; he never wanted to live among the crowds and crime of a metropolitan area again.

So he settled on a bland response. "I had a good time, too."

She removed her seat belt, then turned in the seat until she faced him. "I liked the restaurant very much. I'd forgotten how strong the German influence is here in the Hill Country."

"Most people do, despite the names of the towns that give away the heritage of their founders."

Robin chuckled. "It's been a long time since I took Texas history."

"Not as long as it's been for me."

"You can't be that old."

"Thirty-two, not that I'm counting."

"You're from Texas originally?"

She sounded genuinely interested. Despite his intention to leave as quickly as possible to reduce any chance of acting on his attraction, he wanted to answer her question. "Yes, I grew up in a little town called West."

"I know West. I've shopped for antiques there."

"Then you know it's a lot like the Hill Country in the mix of ethnic backgrounds—Czech, German, English. I didn't appreciate the town too much back then, though. I couldn't wait to get to the big city."

"I suppose most small-town kids are like that."

Ethan nodded. "That's one reason the population of so many rural towns is declining. There aren't many diversions or interesting jobs for young people."

"So you left after high school?"

"I went to college in Fort Worth, then took a job with the FBI. After training, I was assigned to Dallas. I loved it…for about five years."

"Didn't you like your job?"

He shrugged. "I liked most of it. I worked with some good people. I liked the idea of fighting crime, preserving order, that sort of thing. But I did get a little tired of the bureaucracy and paperwork."

"Did you get rid of that when you moved here and became police chief?"

He smiled. "I've done my best to eliminate most of it."

"That's good." She shifted in her seat, smoothing her hair behind one ear. He watched the faint light caress her skin and wanted to do the same with his fingers. Parts of his body wanted to do much, much more.

He felt himself lean forward, the arm that had rested on the top of the steering wheel reaching toward her. As though it were happening in slow motion, he watched her lips part in awareness, her body shift subtly toward his.

He wanted to kiss her. He'd been yearning to taste her lips since she'd cried on her front porch and he'd taken her in his arms. And, apparently, she wanted him to kiss her. All the signs were there. All he had to do was frame her face with his hands and seal his mouth over hers.

The knowledge that she returned his feelings jolted him to attention. He inhaled a deep breath, then eased back in the bucket seat. What was he thinking? Nothing. That was the problem. He'd started acting on primitive instinct, which would prove disastrous. No way could he let this relationship progress from a friendly dinner to a sensual breakfast. No way could he mislead her into thinking he wanted a dating relationship—or anything more.

She must have felt the tension, but he didn't risk looking at her to find out. After a few seconds, she said, "We never did have dessert. Would you like to come in for coffee?"

He made a show of looking at his watch, the dial luminous in the darkness of the interior. "I'd better not. I have to be at the station early in the morning."

"Well, then, thank you for dinner."

He heard the *click* of the door handle and hurried to open his own. The immediate glare of the overhead light further distanced him from the dark, magical moments just passed.

"You don't have to—"

"I'll walk you to your door." He smiled as he came around to her side of the Bronco. "I'm a lawman, remember? Ready to save you from marauding animals or any other threat to your person. Humor me."

"Yes, Chief Parker," she said with a jaunty salute.

He laughed, the tension broken.

"Did I tell you what I originally thought a small-town police chief would look like?" she asked, as they walked up to the porch.

"No, I don't think you mentioned it."

She laughed and shook her head. "I imagined

someone around sixty, looking a lot like Andy Griffith or Carroll O'Connor. I also thought you might have a potbelly and be partial to some sort of tobacco product.''

Ethan laughed at the stereotypical image. ''No potbelly—not yet, anyway.'' He patted his flat stomach, inordinately proud that he'd kept up with his Academy training. ''And no tobacco.''

''Somehow, I just don't see you ever succumbing to stereotype.'' She smiled, but she didn't seem as happy as she had earlier in the evening. He didn't know what to say, so he remained quiet while she unlocked the door.

''Again, I had a good time this evening.''

''I did, too.''

He held on to the storm door, as she stepped inside. He wanted to lean forward, kiss her goodnight. Ask her on another date. But he could do none of those things.

''Good night, Robin.''

''Good night, Ethan.'' She smiled again, then gently closed the door.

He turned and walked quickly back to his Bronco, before he changed his mind and knocked on her door. Before he did something incredibly stupid that Aunt Bess would say was out of line for a first date.

Even for a man who probably got less ''action'' than Bess's friends in the retirement home.

ROBIN WAITED AN ENTIRE DAY to call Ethan. Oh, she'd had second thoughts about contacting him.

And third, and fourth. But she'd promised Bess that she'd spend some time with Ethan, and one dinner date—especially one that ended with him nervously glancing at his watch around ten o'clock at night—probably wouldn't count.

Perhaps he didn't want to spend more time with her. Maybe she'd misread his signals when they were sitting in his Bronco. For a moment, she'd thought he was going to kiss her. She'd responded automatically, before she'd remembered that she was *not* going to get romantically involved.

Of course, even if he had kissed her, that didn't mean they'd develop a relationship. His kisses might not stir her to great passion. Maybe there wasn't any chemistry between them.

Right.

Robin sighed, looking down once again at the business card Ethan had given her at the fast-food restaurant a few days ago. She was trying to fool herself if she thought there was no chemistry. She might be a little rusty from not dating anyone—except her fiancé—for months and months, but she thought she still recognized the signs. It seemed to her that Ethan had been trying awfully hard to be the perfect gentleman during the drive and dinner. That meant one of two things: either he was gritting his teeth and bearing a horrible date, or he was attracted to her and was trying not to show his feelings.

He was a difficult man to read. Obviously, his

FBI and police training served him well. He'd learned to mask his emotions and control his responses more than the average person. She honestly couldn't be sure about Ethan's motives for asking her out in the first place, or for behaving so... properly during their date.

"I owe this to Bess," she told herself as she picked up the phone. She'd promised the older lady, and she wasn't about to disappoint one of her great-aunt's best friends.

She glanced once more at the kitchen clock. Ethan should be home from the police station by now, unless he had someplace else to be. Like a civic function. *Or another date.*

He answered on the third ring. "Hello?"

"Ethan, this is Robin."

She heard him shift the phone, giving them an uncomfortably long pause. "How are you?"

"I'm fine," she said, relieved he sounded at least a little happy to hear from her. She'd been concerned he'd be bored or indifferent, but that's not what she heard in his voice. And she considered herself a good judge of character via the phone lines. After all, she had to read the moods of her clients, and sometimes negotiate the best price for an item with a supplier.

"Ethan, I wanted to tell you again that I enjoyed the drive and dinner the other night."

"I did too, Robin."

"You mentioned your aunt is out of town. I was

wondering if you'd like to come over for dinner tomorrow night.''

"Dinner at your place?"

"Yes, if you'd like."

He paused briefly. She imagined him standing with the phone clutched in one hand, a slight frown on his face. "I don't want you to go to any trouble," he said.

"No problem," she replied, crossing her fingers behind her back. Ethan didn't need to know she couldn't cook. After all, she'd just have to warm up some food she'd purchase. Surely that couldn't be too hard with the new, state-of-the-art cooktop and ovens in the Franklin's French country kitchen. And Mrs. Franklin seemed to have a wide array of pans and dishes. Presenting a meal for two shouldn't be too difficult. At least she felt totally confident of creating a stunning table setting!

"That sounds very nice," he finally said, his voice conveying a deep reservation about accepting.

Robin wanted to put him at ease, so she added, "Please don't think of this as a date. I told you I'd recently broken up with my fiancé. I'm not ready to jump into another relationship. I'd just like to have a friend in town. Nothing more."

"I understand. I agree," he said, sounding relieved.

"Good. I just wanted to be clear about that."

"I appreciate your honesty."

"Okay," she said, releasing a breath. "How about seven o'clock?"

"Sounds good. Can I bring wine?"

"Oh, I'll pick up something when I'm out to-morrow."

"Ranger Springs is dry."

Dry? She'd totally forgotten she was in a rural community, one that obviously didn't want package liquor stores popping up. Just one more difference between country and city life.

"You'd have to drive about fifteen miles," he added. "Why don't I just bring something from home?"

"In that case, thanks. Whatever you'd like will be fine."

"Red or white?"

Hmm. That meant she needed to know what entrée she'd be serving—which was impossible. She had no idea what type of catered food she'd find in Ranger Springs. "Which is your favorite?"

Ethan chuckled. "I'm kind of partial to beer when I drink, which isn't real often."

Robin laughed. "Then bring your favorite beer. I'll try to prepare something appropriate."

"Great. See you tomorrow at seven."

"Good night, Ethan."

She placed the phone gently in the cradle. Well, that wasn't so hard! They'd share a friendly meal. Both of them knew where they stood as far as relationships went. And Bess would be happy that Ethan hadn't died of boredom while she was visiting friends.

What could possibly go wrong?

Chapter Five

"What do you mean, there are no caterers in Ranger Springs?" Robin asked the startled lady at the Chamber of Commerce office the next morning. She knew her voice showed her panic, but she couldn't help herself. Even though she knew the town boasted no mall or fancy restaurants, she'd never considered that she couldn't get a decently prepared meal from some food professional in town.

"You might check at the café. They could fix you some 'to go' food. Their chicken-fried steak is mighty tasty."

"I can't serve chicken-fried steak! No one would believe I fixed that as an entrée!"

Robin knew her voice was rising to near hysteria, but she couldn't believe the situation she'd gotten herself into. Of course, she thought as her gaze darted around the old converted bank building that now housed the Chamber of Commerce, Visitor's Bureau and Historical Society, she shouldn't be surprised. Ranger Springs was a small town, a down-home, Texas-y place, where chicken-fried steak was considered the best a restaurant could offer. How could she have forgotten where she was staying when she'd invited Ethan to dinner tonight?

Tonight! She had to get busy.

"Or you could wait until next Wednesday night," the middle aged lady offered. "The Methodist church has a covered dish supper once a month. All the women bring their best. You'd be sure to get some good food there."

"I'm sure I would," Robin replied, her tone reflecting her despair. But she wasn't going to accomplish anything by panicking. She'd just have to come up with another plan.

"How about the grocery stores. Do they sell prepared foods?"

The woman appeared confused. "I don't think so, unless you mean those frozen dinners."

"No, I'm talking about rotisserie chicken, spiral cut hams, that sort of thing?"

"I've never seen anything like that. Most of the women in town fix their own chickens. Well, not real live chickens, mind you. You can get good fryers or roasters at the grocery store."

Robin rested her chin in her hand as she leaned against the high counter. "How long does it take to drive to Austin or San Antonio?"

"About an hour to the outskirts of San Antonio, about forty-five minutes to the Austin area."

"Okay. They'll have caterers."

"I suppose so." The woman tilted her head to the side, then asked, "You really don't cook?"

"Not much." And what she did cook rarely turned out looking like the recipe or tasting like the dish she was trying to imitate—even though she never tried anything elaborate or difficult. Her mother didn't cook, and Great-aunt Sylvia limited her kitchen time to an occasional batch of cookies. Robin had accepted the fact she'd never be a cook, although she could set an elegant and innovative table.

"Thank you," Robin told the nice lady who still looked confused. "I'd appreciate it if you wouldn't mention this to anyone. I'm not going to be in town for very long, but it's kind of embarrassing for others to know I can't fix a decent meal." *Especially the chief of police or his nice aunt,* she silently added.

Robin slipped on her sunglasses and stepped into the Texas summer heat. She unlocked the car, let the hot air escape, then sat down in the cushy driver's seat. She'd calmed down; there was no reason to panic. She could get what she needed and still be back by one o'clock.

The evening would be pleasant. She'd explain to Ethan again that she only thought of him as a friend; she wasn't looking for a romantic relationship. She'd thank him for making her feel welcome in town, and send him on his way. No awkward scenes at the front door. No near-kisses in the car or on the porch.

Absolutely not. As soon as she had this food situation under control, she'd feel much more in-charge when it came to Ethan Parker and his reluctant, sexy smiles. And his bedroom eyes. And his to-die-for body.

All she needed was some good food and fresh flowers. She'd do what she did best: create a relaxing and decorative environment. Then everything would be fine.

ROBIN HAD DECIDED on a summer theme of red, white and blue. Using Mrs. Franklin's casual white fluted place settings and her pistol-grip handle flatware, she'd had set the table with blue and white toile place mats. At a lovely shop in Dripping Springs, a suburb of Austin, she'd found red gingham napkins which she folded in a *fleur-de-lis* shape. Then she'd gathered blue Delft pottery from around the house and created a centerpiece of Texas bluebonnets, white delphinia and red tulips from a florist shop in the same suburb where she'd located a gourmet restaurant that catered.

Of course, she'd spent entirely too much time shopping, and too much money on the new-potato salad, roasted chicken, risotto and marinated string beans. That hadn't stopped her from buying for dessert an adorable blueberry, strawberry and whipped cream confection in the design of an American flag.

"Perfect," she said, adjusting the last tulip so it draped artfully over the edge of the blue-and-white pottery. All she had to do was light the two white tapers and the setting would be suitable for a Fourth of July *Traditional Home* photo shoot.

She'd enjoyed the preparations and the decorating. But how was she going to get through the next weeks without the adrenaline high of searching for caterers in a small town? Or preparing for a special guest? Or having a relaxing and fun evening with a...friend?

She'd wanted to get away from friends and family, but she hadn't really thought through the reality of living alone in a town where she knew no one. Or practically no one. Bess and Ethan were the only two people she could call close acquaintances, and the older lady only because of Great-aunt Sylvia.

She was going to get darn lonely. And broke. Since she'd cleared her professional commitments in preparation for the wedding, she had no money coming in. What was left in her checking account should have lasted two months, if she'd been careful. But she'd foolishly blown her weekly budget on food, flowers and napkins for one night. Why? Was she so lonely for company that she'd courted Ethan's approval and attention?

Under regular circumstances, with her normal income, she could have filled countless days scouring antique stores, flea markets and garage sales throughout the area. But not with her present finances! How, she wondered, was she going to fill up her days and nights without work, shopping or friends?

The fact that she hadn't included her former fiancé in her thoughts was another indication she'd done the right thing by calling off the wedding. If she'd been madly in love with Gig Harrelson, she would be missing him terribly. All she felt was an enormous sense of relief. Her reason for marrying him was wrong, and she would have realized it earlier if she'd allowed herself to step back and think about their relationship. Yes, she still missed the familiarity, but not the particular man with whom she had nearly pledged to spend the rest of her life.

She was learning a lot about herself, but she was also going to get lonesome before long. She might have to return to Houston early, even though she'd signed a contract with the real estate agent to stay in the house two months. Funny thing was, she really didn't want to go back to her condo, to her life, just yet. She'd rather enjoyed her temporary stay in Ranger Springs so far. She'd continue enjoying it if she had a little more money and she could remain friends with Ethan. And spend time with Bess, when the older woman returned from San Antonio.

Robin just had to remember to treat Ethan exactly as she did his elderly aunt.

She smiled as she straightened, thinking that she needed a little time to freshen up before Ethan arrived. She'd focused almost all her attention on the table, telling herself her appearance wasn't all that important. After all, she wasn't trying to attract Ethan's attention. She certainly didn't want to appear as polished and perfect as her table setting. She simply wanted to be…neat. Clean. She didn't want to look like she'd been rushing around all afternoon like a madwoman.

When she glanced at her watch, however, she realized "freshening up" might consist of patting the perspiration off her forehead and running a brush through her hair. Ethan was scheduled to arrive in ten minutes, and she assumed the food would be warm by then.

As if thinking about dinner had made it a reality, the smell of scorching vegetables wafted through the open kitchen doorway. She recognized the odor immediately; her cooking usually took on this particular odor before she dumped it down the garbage disposal.

"Darn it," she muttered, rushing into the spacious kitchen and jerking open the oven. The roasted chicken was hissing at her from inside the hot interior, and the string beans had shriveled into wrinkled green ropes in the middle of a large but attractive enamel pot on the stove. She pulled the pot off the burner just as the doorbell rang—and noticed that she'd totally forgotten to warm the risotto.

"Great. He's early," she mumbled as she pulled the sputtering chicken from the oven. The skin of the roasted bird seemed to have a life of its own as steam escaped from various crannies. "Yuck." She should have chosen a nice, quiet chicken breast filet instead of this whole bird, which seemed reluctant to make it to the table.

The doorbell rang again. Using the kitchen towel,

Robin patted her face and neck, straightened her mid-calf-length sundress and ran both hands through her hair. Ethan would just have to face her as she was; she didn't have time for even minimal primping. She rushed toward the entryway.

"Hello," she said breathlessly as she opened the door.

"Hi," he said, his eyes skimming her quickly. "You look great." He immediately clamped his mouth shut, as though he'd already said too much.

Robin grinned. Despite saying she wasn't going to get involved, despite assurances to him and to herself that she wasn't ready for any kind of romantic relationship, there was nothing like a good-looking man's appreciative stare to make a woman feel good. And heavens, Ethan did look good tonight in a solid, dark red shirt and body-hugging jeans. He was one-hundred percent Texas male, from his regulation haircut to his worn-but-shiny cowboy boots. Yes, this man's compliment made her pulse race and her palms itch.

Even if she did have a hissing chicken and stringy beans waiting to bring her back to reality.

TWO THINGS HIT Ethan simultaneously as soon as he tore his attention away from Robin: first, the house—specifically the dining room—looked like something from one of those fancy decorating magazines Susie, his daytime dispatcher, provided for the police department waiting room; and second, it smelled like something from his early college days when he was still learning to scorch his meals to bachelorhood perfection.

"Please, come in," Robin said, her voice breathless and sexy as hell. He didn't suppose she meant to sound like she'd just had a satisfying roll in the hay. But darn it, she looked like she'd been caught doing something very naughty and pleasurable, and he couldn't help it if his mind automatically jumped to conclusions. Her cheeks were flushed a deep pink, her eyes were sparkling and a damp sheen made her filmy sundress cling to every curve of her body.

"I'm a mess," she apologized as she walked into the living room, talking over her shoulder. "I do this all the time; I get carried away with decorating and forget I have other things to do." She pushed a strand of hair behind her ear as she stopped beside the couch. "I meant to freshen up a little before you arrived."

"I'm probably early. And you look...fine."

"Thanks," she said with a laugh. "That's very gentlemanly of you."

"It's the least I can say after showing up before you were expecting me."

Robin laughed. "If I tell my friends in Houston seven o'clock, most of them will show up from seven-fifteen to seven-thirty. A few might even stretch it to eight."

"That's one of the differences between the city and the country," Ethan replied, presenting a bag that contained a six-pack of his favorite beer, plus something for her. "Can I put this in the refrigerator?"

"I'll take it." Her hands brushed over his as she tried to scoop the heavy bag into her arms.

"Let me," he said at the same time.

She laughed, relinquishing her hold, as he tried to control his reaction to her innocent and fleeting touch. Man, he was in trouble if he couldn't get through the first few minutes without thinking about how sexy she looked and sounded, and how he wanted to be the reason her cheeks were flushed and her breathing was shallow.

"Follow me."

Gladly, he silently answered, as she breezed into the kitchen. Her hips swayed ever so slightly. Only her lower calves and ankles were visible beneath the hem of her sundress. But to him, the sight was very arousing.

She opened the side-by-side refrigerator, gesturing inside. "Put it anywhere it will fit."

"I brought some white wine for you. I wasn't sure if you were a beer drinker."

"Thanks. I'd love a glass of wine. I didn't bring any with me when I left Houston. I forgot how difficult it was to find a store out in the boonies... Sorry. I didn't mean to sound disparaging of your town. I like it very much. Really."

He handed her the bottle of chardonnay, then extracted a bottle of beer for himself. "No problem. I like being out in the boonies." But her comments had reinforced one of their main differences—big city and small town, just like wine and beer, didn't mix. No matter how attractive he found Robin, he had to keep that fact in mind.

"I'll get you a glass."

"Not necessary," he said, twisting off the cap. "Can I get the cork for you?"

"I'll do it. Just make yourself at home."

She searched in two drawers before she found the corkscrew. "I'm still getting used to the house."

"I'm sure it's very different from your place in Houston."

"Very. I live in a high-rise condo without much storage. My kitchen cabinets hold a small set of dinnerware and a wide variety of glasses—I admit I eat most meals out. And my drawers aren't full of all the gadgets Mrs. Franklin obviously uses."

"So you're not really into cooking."

She froze, looking at him with wide eyes. Then she bestowed a big, fake smile and said, "Not as much as I'm into decorating."

Ethan smiled in reply, speculating that her remark was a huge understatement. Somehow, the knowledge that she'd gone to so much trouble to fix dinner for him when she obviously didn't enjoy cooking made the evening more special. For a special *friend,* he reminded himself. Ever since her phone call yesterday, he'd told himself many times how grateful he was that she'd made her intentions known up front. He'd been very worried that Robin wanted more of a romantic relationship than he could give her.

"Let me help. If you'll show me where the lids are, I'll try to keep the chicken and green beans warm while we relax a moment. You look as if you could use a glass of wine."

"That obvious, huh?" she said with amusement in her voice. Her smile changed to a frown. "Lids. I'm not sure—"

"I'll look," Ethan offered. He had no trouble locating them in Mrs. Franklin's well-organized and equipped kitchen. Within a few moments, he and Robin both had a cold drink and had headed into the living room.

He'd been nervous about coming to dinner tonight, but now he was glad he'd accepted Robin's invitation. She was lonely, just as her aunt had said, even if she *had* wanted him to kiss her last night in the Bronco. Her reaction was probably an abnormality, brought on by the night, her loneliness, and who knew what other emotions. He'd never been great at reading women. If he'd been more in tune to their moods and needs, he wouldn't be sitting here with Robin tonight. He'd be with someone else—in a much more permanent situation.

His first impression of Robin as a hard-hearted man-killer who thought nothing of leaving her fiancé at the altar was as wrong as could be. Given his background, though, how could anyone blame him for being suspicious? Thank heavens he wouldn't have to relive any of those painful memories, especially since he and Robin were going to be just friends.

"SO THAT'S WHAT decorators do," Robin said, finishing her glass of wine. They'd cleared the table and disposed of the remains of the overdone-but-tasty dinner. What had been left wasn't salvageable for leftovers—not that Robin looked like the type of woman who saved leftovers. She seemed like the sort who preferred catered meals and restaurant fare—and Ethan didn't mean fast food. He and Robin were as different as armadillos and rattle-snakes.

"So you do what the client wants," Ethan said as he sat beside her—but not too close—on the couch.

"Well, within reason. For example, if I had a client who wanted a nubby beige sofa, white walls and 'starving artist' oil paintings, I'd advise them against using me as a decorator. They can get that sort of thing at any furniture store."

Ethan cringed inwardly. Aunt Bess didn't seem to mind their decor, which *had* pretty much come from the local furniture store, and the white walls, which had been painted just prior to his buying the one-story, ranch-style home on two acres of land. He'd picked the house because of its location near the main road—rural but not far from the municipal building—and the fact there weren't steps for Aunt Bess to climb. Since moving to Ranger Springs, he'd rarely thought about how the house looked inside.

Of course, he wanted a well-kept yard, which he mowed and trimmed weekly. The interior always seemed to him the domain of the "woman of the house," and in his case, that was his elderly aunt. If he'd gotten married a few years ago, he might not spend his evenings in his comfortable lounger with his aunt sitting on the nubby beige sofa beneath the cheap oil painting of sea grass on a sandy dune.

"So what if a client already had that sort of style and wanted something else? What would you do?"

"I'd ask them what they liked, what kind of lifestyle they lived, how long they were going to be in the house, and what budget they were considering. Then I could come up with some preliminary ideas. Many clients enjoy shopping with me at design centers, antique stores and specialty shops for ideas and accessories." She paused. "If I were in Houston, of course. I haven't even seen an antique store in Ranger Springs."

He'd always thought the fact that Ranger Springs *didn't* have an antique store was a point in its favor, but he supposed Robin wouldn't appreciate his opinion. Most of the stuff he'd seen inside those stores, on the two occasions he'd gone with his aunt, looked to him like someone else's discards. "So you wouldn't hold it against the client if they didn't have a lot of stylish furniture and…knick-knacks to begin with?"

Robin laughed. "No, I wouldn't. The most important thing is that the client and I can agree on a strategy for improving the look and function of their home."

"Sounds like a big job."

"I think so. People make fun of decorators, but we enjoy helping people live in a better environment. Some decorators work very closely with energy-saving and earth-friendly products, or with architects who design state-of-the-art houses. Most clients don't want their homes to look like computer workstations or industrial sites."

"I can understand that. I like a real homey look myself, but I have a hard time knowing what that means, exactly." He took a sip of iced tea, enjoying the low-key conversation more than he'd imagined. "It's like a lot of things—you just know it when you see it."

Robin laughed. "Believe me, I've heard that before, especially from male clients. Women tend to be more opinionated and have a better idea of their personal style."

And some of them have a hard time admitting what they really want out of life, he thought. But again, he was thinking of his past, which had no bearing on the present. He couldn't lump Robin in with other women he'd known.

"Do most of your clients want something modern? Bright colors and glass cubes and things like that?" he asked.

"Actually, most people want a fairly traditional

look, but they want to make their statement, too. For example, they might have inherited fine cherry or mahogany dining room furniture, but they collect modern art. It's easy for a decorator to combine the two to make a striking room, but it takes skill and confidence some home-owners don't possess. Success comes from color and balance. Convincing a client to paint their walls dark red is a real challenge,'' she added with a chuckle.

''Most people around here don't collect modern art,'' he observed.

''No, but I'll bet a lot of them have some fine antiques that they've either inherited or purchased. Some people have trouble integrating those pieces with their existing furniture.'' She finished her glass of wine, then smiled. ''Why? Do you think Ranger Springs could use a decorator?''

He narrowed his eyes and studied her, trying to imagine her setting up shop in a small town. The possibilities were slim, so he settled on ''Maybe.''

She shook her head. ''I doubt it. A lot of people see decorators as an added expense they simply don't need. They're happy with their beige sofas and white walls.''

''But what if they're not? Wouldn't you like to help?''

''I'm almost always willing to help...for commission or a fee,'' she said with a smile.

''How about my house? Would you help me get rid of the furniture-store look?''

"Your house?" She seemed to still, like a leaf momentarily caught in an updraft.

"Sure. I don't know anything about decorating. Aunt Bess is as sweet as can be, but she's happy with whatever pleases me. Oh, she's got some antiques in her bedroom—a lot of knickknacks from her family. But they're hers, not mine. Honestly, I think she's kind of stuck in the sixties or seventies from what she said when we went shopping a few years ago. I'm beginning to think I need help."

"You're serious."

"Very." Hiring Robin to decorate his house would keep her busy, so she wouldn't be lonely. And if he gave her free rein to buy all those little things that made a place look like a home, she'd be working and out of his hair during the day. He wouldn't have to worry about her sitting alone in this big house with nothing to do but think about her friends and family—and ex-fiancé—back in Houston. And best of all, he'd get the kind of home he'd always wanted, but couldn't decorate on his own.

Surely his aunt would agree that hiring Robin to decorate was an even better inspiration than taking her out to dinner or a movie.

He could tell Robin was seriously considering the offer. She didn't hide her feelings very well; he had no idea whether she could conceal her emotions even if she tried.

Her eyes sparkled as she leaned slightly toward

him. "I'd like to see your house and discuss what you want."

Ethan shrugged. "Sure, but it's pretty standard stuff. One-story brick, three bedrooms, two baths. And as for what I want, I'm not really sure. I just want to make it more...homey. You know, kind of personal but not too fussy. I don't like fussy. No frilly lace curtains and tiny little chairs. And I'm not giving up my recliner or big-screen TV."

Robin laughed. "Somehow, I could have guessed that."

BEFORE LONG, ETHAN announced he needed to get home. He had to work tomorrow, but at least this evening hadn't ended like the one two nights ago, with him looking at his watch with a panicked expression on his face. No, tonight he'd appeared relaxed and pleased.

"I enjoyed the dinner," he said, as she opened the door for him.

"Even if it was a little overcooked."

"Just a bit," he said, smiling in the appealing way she'd appreciated from the very beginning. She suspected he wasn't the type of man who smiled a lot at work, given his status as chief of police and his FBI training. But he had a lot of warmth inside. She could tell by the way he treated his aunt, and the way he offered a smile as if he wasn't sure it would be accepted.

"I'll need to have a look at your house. In the meantime, I'll get my sample books and try to line up some local resources for whatever work you'd like to have done.''

"Work?'' He sounded worried.

"Painting or simple woodwork,'' she clarified. "I didn't mean you'd want major remodeling.''

"Oh. Good.'' He sighed in relief. "Why don't you come by this weekend? I have Saturday and Sunday off. Aunt Bess and I were planning on working in the yard, but since she's in San Antonio, I have both days free.''

"I'll come by Saturday, then. Around ten o'clock?''

"Sounds good.'' He smiled again as he opened the storm door and stepped out onto the porch. "I'll see you Saturday.''

"Good night, Ethan.''

"Good night.'' He paused, his smile fading a little as he looked at her across the few feet that separated them. "I really did have a good time.''

She tilted her head and hugged her arms. "I did, too.''

He nodded, then smiled again. She wondered briefly if he was going to do or say something else. But he turned and walked to his black Bronco, his long-legged, rolling stride reminding her much more of an old-time Texas lawman than a modern, FBI-trained cop.

She shook off her fanciful thoughts and locked the door, closing out the warm summer night and the vision of Ethan Parker. She had things to do—

important tasks related to the work she loved. First of all, she had to make a list.

She hadn't needed to set up a work center in the Franklin home; she hadn't expected to work while she was here in Ranger Springs. But now she'd need paper, pencils, a sketchbook and all the tools of her trade that were back in the small office she shared with her partner, Jenny Smithson.

Fortunately, Robin had been at the end of her current projects because of the impending wedding. Only a few details and minor problems had to be resolved. Jenny had graciously agreed to take care of those remnants when she'd received Robin's phone call, briefly revealing her retreat from Houston.

They weren't close friends, but they complemented each other well in a professional sense. Jenny had a wonderful sense of the absurd; Robin had the ability to take the traditional elements of design and use them individually.

Her talent, she'd learned over the four years she'd been a professional decorator, was integrating a client's collection into a total decorating scheme.

She paused, wondering if Ethan had any "collections." Somehow, she doubted it, unless he had items from his childhood.

She found a yellow pad and pencil in one of the drawers in the kitchen. Taking a seat at the breakfast nook, she began to list what she knew—what she thought she knew—about Ethan. The exercise would be helpful in more ways than one. By accepting him as a client, she could look at him objectively. No longer would he be the sexy chief of police, nor would he be the nonsexual friend she'd tried to envision. Now he could be a real man—a client—with an expressed personality, goals and preferences. She could list those attributes, weigh them and analyze them.

In short, she could control her reaction to Ethan once he was reduced to a series of words on a piece of paper. The idea invigorated her. She experienced the sort of excitement she always felt when she took on a difficult or challenging task.

Purely professional, she told herself. Thinking of excitement and Ethan in the same context was only inviting trouble if she failed to remember he was a client, just like any other.

Pencil poised above the yellow pad, she began listing Ethan's personality traits. *Strong. Responsible. Punctual.*

She rubbed the bridge of her nose. The word *sexy* kept popping into her mind, but she had to find another way to express it. *Desirable.* Definitely, but that hardly helped her keep her mind off the personal and on the professional. *Appealing.* Now there was a thought. He appealed to many people, she was sure, for his various abilities and his position in the community. The fact that he appealed to her on many levels was irrelevant; he was a bundle of tantalizing traits anyone would recognize.

She worked on the list for a few more minutes, adding words as they came to her: *down-home, hon-*

est, country boy, educated, law-abiding, good-natured, Texan. In the end, she had about fifteen words and phrases that began to define Ethan Parker.

She couldn't wait to start the project. She'd be required to spend plenty of time around him, but suddenly the prospect wasn't scary. Now that he was a client, she wouldn't have to worry about wild attraction or almost-kisses.

In bold strokes she printed "The Bachelor Project" on the top of the yellow sheet of paper. Now she had a project title, a real client and a plan of action.

For the first time since he'd answered her 9-1-1 call, she felt as if both her feet were firmly on the ground. Ethan would love her ideas for his home, she was sure. If he hadn't wanted to spend time with her, have her help define his style and reveal his preferences for particular purchases, he certainly wouldn't have asked her to redecorate his house. No one made that sort of commitment on a whim.

Yes, her stay in Ranger Springs was definitely looking up. Perhaps she'd be able to afford more than frozen dinners and an occasional fast-food burger. After tonight, she was more convinced than ever that she wasn't going to be forced to learn to cook simply because she was living in the midst of Americana.

The country wasn't going to rub off on a city girl like her, but with some skill and perseverance, a little bit of the city was about to rub off on Ranger Springs's police chief.

Chapter Six

"Thank you so much for the references, Mr. Branson," Robin said the next morning. The hardware store manager had been very helpful, supplying her with several names of individuals who painted and did light carpentry work. Between locating the business cards of the contractors, he'd waited on several people and answered questions ranging from fence stretchers to plumbing fittings to satin versus high-gloss paint finishes. She'd have to remember this quaint small-town experience when she returned to Houston.

"Call me Jimmy Mack," the man said. "Near ever'body does."

Robin smiled and shook his hand. "Thank you, Jimmy Mack. I'll be in touch for whatever supplies I need."

Before she could start for the door, he commented, "The Franklins jus' had their house fixed up before they left."

"I know. It's a lovely home."

"You buyin' a place here in town?"

"No, I'm not." Before he could continue, she said, "I really have to go. Thanks again for the references." She hated to turn her back on him and walk away, but she absolutely would not divulge the name of her client. There was nothing peculiar or irresponsible about updating decor, but the business was between herself and her client. If Jimmy Mack mentioned the exact reason she needed painters and carpenters to friends, someone in Ranger Springs might make an issue out of her working on Ethan's house, especially with his aunt out of town. She assumed most of the people around here were as curious as the hardware manager.

Robin headed across the town square to the flooring store. She wasn't sure if she could get a good price on wall-to-wall carpet, if that's what Ethan wanted. Personally, she loved natural hardwoods and tile, but not everyone could be convinced the extra money was worthwhile. If he decided against carpet, she couldn't be sure a store that small would have a decent selection of area rugs. But she'd try to use local sources whenever possible. If necessary, she and Ethan could travel to Austin or San Antonio. Even the market in Dallas wasn't out of the question, as far as she was concerned.

The idea of spending time alone with him, traveling in his Bronco or her small, sporty coupe, shouldn't make her heart rate increase. She shouldn't allow herself to have such a response to a client. In the past, the problem hadn't arisen;

she'd never felt the least attraction to any of her male employers.

Of course, she'd been engaged for the past year and a half, and seriously dating Gig for months before then. Being in a committed relationship was enough to stop most people from acknowledging desire for someone else, but Robin doubted even her engagement would have kept her from seeing Ethan as a very sexy man. Even more reason to keep her personal feelings firmly in control.

She avoided the cracked sidewalk in front of a movie theater that had been closed since the first "Die Hard" movie had premiered. The faded poster rested wearily beneath the glass next to a hand-printed schedule. The boarded up box office seemed sad, as though waiting for someone to tear away the covering and thread a film through the projector once more.

Crossing the street, she headed for the Four Square Café. A sandwich and iced tea sounded great. She'd been running on adrenaline since she'd talked to Jenny earlier this morning. As soon as she entered the old-fashioned eatery, she saw the sign that proclaimed Please Seat Yourself, and started walking between tables and booths, causing almost every head in the place to turn. Smiling vaguely, she located a red vinyl booth near the rear and slipped across the squeaky seat.

She supposed the "new kid" in town always caused extra attention, but she was more familiar with the discreet, assessing looks that certain striking individuals or celebrities caused in the trendy restaurants she frequented in Houston's better sections. She'd never thought of herself as a snob, but she had to admit that she wouldn't choose a restaurant like this one if she had a choice.

She *always* had a choice, she reminded herself. She could go back to town anytime she wanted, face the questions and uncomfortable social situations and get on with her life. But she wasn't ready...and besides, she'd begun to like the small town, even though the food, people and businesses were radically different from what she was used to.

"Robin!"

She turned to see Gina Mae Summers, the real estate agent who had handled the agreement to house-sit the Franklin's home. Dressed in a bright coral sleeveless top and matching slacks, she looked fashionable and summery. Robin smiled and motioned her over.

"Would you like to join me? I just sat down."

"I'd love to." Gina placed her purse and planner on the seat and scooted to the center of the red booth. "Are you enjoying the house?"

"Very much. It's a lovely place."

"I heard you had some unexpected visitors the other night," Gina said in a conspiratorial tone.

"Visitors? Oh, you mean the raccoons. You must have been talking to Eth—Police Chief Parker." The idea of the attractive real estate agent and the sexy lawman talking together caused an unexpected pang in Robin's midsection. *Just because they were talking about me,* she told herself.

"Yes. As a matter of fact, he saw me in this very restaurant and was asking about you."

"Really." Robin frowned. "What in the world would he want to know about me?"

"Nothing official, if that's what you're thinking. I believe his interest was more…personal."

"No, that's—" Robin paused. "What makes you think so?"

Gina shrugged. "The way he tried so hard to make his questions sound official. The man was trying too much to convince me he was just checking up on the house."

"I'm sure he was interested to discover who was living there."

"Yes, he was doing his job. But I've been around long enough to tell the difference between official duties and personal attention. Believe me, Ethan Parker found you a lot more interesting than a few curious raccoons."

"He's a very nice man, but there's nothing going on. Nothing personal," Robin added. She wasn't about to confess that she and Ethan had gone to dinner in Wimberley, that they'd had a meal at her place, and that she was currently working on decorating his house.

Gina studied her over the dog-eared menu. "Whatever you say."

"Believe me, I'm not getting involved with anyone. I just left a long-term relationship, and the last thing I want is to find myself attracted to a man in a small town where I'm staying for such a short time.''

"I understand."

Robin nodded, still not certain she'd convinced Gina of her intentions. However, hunger and good manners prevented her from speaking any more about the strictly professional relationship she shared with Ethan. When the waitress came to their booth, she ordered a club sandwich and iced tea. She only hoped she could keep tongues from wagging over what was sure to be a nonissue—even for a small town that obviously enjoyed good gossip.

ETHAN TOSSED his running shoes into his closet, then shut the door. The house was as picked-up as it was going to get. He was fairly certain Robin would be too busy noticing his lack of decorating sense to comment on his housekeeping skills. Not that he was a slob. He just wasn't obsessive about making sure the fringe on the rug in the entry was combed in one direction. Once she saw his house, any romantic notions she could have mustered would be gone in a flash. She'd know that he and she were as mismatched as delicate china and hand-made pottery.

The doorbell rang as he walked through the living room. Robin was right on time.

"Hello," he said as he answered the door. He gave her a quick glance from the top of her sleek hair to the light pink polish on the toes peeking out from her sandals. Very cute toes, he added—not that he should be noticing any part of her anatomy. Her eyes sparkled in anticipation, and she was, to be honest, far too lovely to be just a friendly decorator.

He hadn't seen her in days, he told himself. That's why he was reacting to her in a slightly less than professional manner. And that had to be the only reason. Memories of his past failed relationships put a damper on any notions he might have about Robin. He wasn't going to repeat his mistakes, not even for someone as appealing as the woman standing before him.

"Hi." She carried a bundle of notebooks, magazines and papers.

"Can I help with those?"

"No, thanks. I'm used to carrying around my office, although usually I have a nice leather satchel. I forgot to ask my partner to send it along with the rest of my supplies."

"I hope I didn't make you go to too much trouble. I hadn't thought about what you might need to start this whole decorating process." He frowned as he motioned for her to place her materials on the heavy oak coffee table that had supported his feet through many ball games. Before he'd gotten the mammoth recliner, he'd owned a sofa that was as disreputable as it was comfortable. The coffee table had matched that couch real well.

Damn, he hoped Robin didn't suggest one of those sissy tables with legs resembling toothpicks.

Or one of those uptight, upright couches covered in material that you were afraid to sit on.

"No problem. I hope we can come to an agreement. I'm excited about the prospect of decorating your home. In fact, I've already asked around town for painters and carpenters, in case we agree on certain changes."

He sat beside her on the sofa, suddenly nervous about this whole idea. If word got around that he'd hired some fancy Houston decorator to fix up his house, he'd never hear the end of it from his employees and friends. Especially the men on the city council, who had even less sense of style than he possessed.

"You didn't happen to mention why you needed the names, did you?"

"Of course not. I keep my relationship with a client private, unless they care to tell their friends."

"I'm just not sure how the guys at the VFW post or the feed store will take the news that the chief of police is picking out wallpaper."

Robin laughed. "Believe me, I understand. My lips are sealed."

Her innocent comment immediately brought his attention to her mouth. Her beautifully shaped, expressive, all-too-kissable mouth. Shaking himself out of a totally inappropriate response—like pushing her down on the nubby beige sofa and kissing her until neither of them were thinking of color or style or what his friends would say about new drapes. The image made him shift uncomfortably on the normally relaxing couch. *Think of something else,* he told himself. *Baseball. Accident scenes. Anything but Robin's lips.*

But like the proverbial elephant in the corner, once brought to his attention, he could barely think of anything else. *Be professional. Be friendly. Stop acting like a horny teenager.*

He coughed discreetly, then said, "Well, let's see what you have there. I'm ready to get started."

Boy, was he ready.

ROBIN SELF-CONSCIOUSLY paced off the measurements of Ethan's living room and adjoining dining room. She felt his gaze on her wherever she went. She'd also seen his slight frown and the worried expression he wore when he didn't think she was looking. On a purely feminine level, she realized he wasn't concerned about her decorating prowess. No, he was concerned about his reaction to her.

Not good. Not when she'd finally conquered her personal attraction to him and was ready to get on with business.

She stopped and chewed her lip as she wrote down the width of the dining room. Okay, maybe not *conquered,* but she'd made some huge leaps in that direction. So what if her pulse had leaped when he'd opened the door dressed in soft, faded jeans and an equally faded San Antonio Spurs championship T-shirt? So what if she'd arrived prematurely and had to drive around for five minutes to keep from ringing his doorbell unfashionably early?

She was anxious to start the project, not to see Ethan. She'd decided, and by golly, she was going to stick to this decision!

She'd already backed down on one of her commitments lately. She wasn't about to start changing her mind again, even if the first, the most major, change had been the right one: stopping her wedding to Gig.

"About finished?" Ethan asked, bringing her attention back to him.

She turned toward the couch and smiled. "Yes, I've completed the measurements. Now we can talk about your ideas."

"I don't have many ideas…about decorating," he added, as she sat beside him on the couch. She would have taken a chair across from him, but the only one available was a huge recliner that looked as if it would swallow her whole. Since it was positioned directly in front of the big-screen television, she assumed this was Ethan's "throne" during his hours off.

"Surely you've seen something in the magazines you liked," she said, indicating the small stack she'd left on the coffee table while she'd looked around and measured the rooms. She knew perfectly well he'd barely studied the decorating journals, but she wasn't about to let him off the hook. She wanted this job to be a joint effort, not some stylistic approach she decided on her own. Unless her clients specifically said they had no ideas and did not want to become involved, she preferred to suggest options and get input from them on the place where they'd be living.

"Um," he said, his gaze fixed on her mouth for the tenth time since she'd arrived at his house. "I really didn't look that closely…at the magazines," he finished, turning his attention back to the selections she'd brought.

You might have, if you'd been paying attention to the decorating, not the decorator, she silently admonished. "Let's look at them together, then," she suggested, scooting a bit closer and picking up her favorite that contained an article on Texas-style furnishings. The photos had been taken not far from here, in another small town, Bandera. The decorator had overdone the cowboy chic, Robin suspected, because that's what New York editors and transplanted northerners expected from a Texas designer. Still, there were many good ideas to consider.

"What do you think about this?" Robin asked, turning to the marked page.

"Aunt Bess wouldn't like it," he said bluntly.

"What do you think?"

"I'd feel like I was sitting in the middle of a theme restaurant."

Robin laughed. "I know what you mean. How about if there were fewer branding irons and less movie memorabilia? Would you like it then?"

Ethan made a face she could only describe as cautiously disparaging. "No, I don't think so. I guess it would be fine for a little boy's room, but not for me.''

"Now I'm going to have to accuse you of being a male chauvinist. I'll have you know little girls like Western themes, too."

"Okay, I get your point. But I'm not a child, and I think this is too fussy in the leather-denim-rusty horseshoe style."

Robin laughed. "Fair enough." She put the magazine back on the stack. She didn't need Ethan's reminders that he wasn't a child. The more time she spent around him, the more adult male he became. Luckily, he was an adult male *client*.

She selected a magazine containing a French country motif she liked. The furniture was solid enough for a man like Ethan, but there were decorative touches his aunt would like, as well. "Take a look at this."

He didn't wrinkle his nose this time, but he didn't appear excited by the style, either. "I'm not sure. There's still a lot of…stuff in the room."

"So you'd rather stay with a more open arrangement."

"I suppose." He looked as though he was getting a headache.

She placed the magazine on the stack and straightened them, then turned to Ethan. "Why don't I leave these with you so you can take a look at your leisure? Just mark the pages of anything you like, whether it's a lamp or a couch or a paint color.

When we get together next time, we'll look over your selections.''

"When are we getting together again?" he asked quietly, his gaze straying once more to her mouth, then back to her eyes.

She drew in a breath, reminding herself not to think anything of Ethan's awareness. He probably behaved this way around all women. He was just a sexy guy. He couldn't help it if his natural expressions made a woman go weak in the knees and lose her train of thought.

"The sooner the better," she heard herself say, then closed her eyes in embarrassment. The words had come out breathy, suggestive. "I mean—because we're working on a tight schedule, we have to make some decisions soon."

"Because you're not going to be in town very long," he said, his own expression changing to a more businesslike one.

"Exactly. I'm planning on staying through July." Unless she ignored her own advice and messed up her friendly, professional relationship with Ethan. She had no intention of allowing this unwanted and inappropriate reaction to escalate. Because if she did something wild and crazy, like revealing her attraction to the sexy bachelor, she'd *have* to leave with her tail tucked between her legs.

"How about tomorrow, then? Come around one o'clock, and I'll fix us something to eat after church. Aunt Bess stocked the freezer with meals, and there's plenty for two."

"I'm not sure—"

"She'll be upset if she comes home and finds a full freezer. Besides, I'm certain she'd want her best friend's great-niece to have a little company."

The aunts again. How could she say no to such logic? "Only if you promise to study those magazines. We have to decide on a style. Oh, and if you have any collections, from baseball memorabilia to Christmas ornaments, show me tomorrow. A theme or focal point would go a long way toward getting us started."

"I'm not much of a collector."

"Whatever you have. Think about it."

"I will." His gaze strayed once more to her lips, then he jerked his head around and pushed himself up from the sofa. "Thank you for coming over."

"You're welcome. I'm looking forward to the project."

He stood with his hands on his hips, staring at the awful oil painting over the couch. "I imagine you are."

Robin smiled. "You could have a yard sale when we're finished."

"I think I'll donate it to the new community center."

"They'll be thrilled," Robin said, tongue in cheek.

"Don't get smart with me," he teased, "or I'll decide this painting absolutely has to stay."

"A theme of sand dunes and pastels." Robin pursed her lips and tapped a finger against her mouth. "I can see it now—seashell plant hangers, ceiling-high sea grasses, pinkish-beige walls and carpet. Of course, we'll need to install a large aquarium in the wall."

"Very funny." He chuckled as they walked toward the door. "I'll see what I can find so we don't get stuck with cheesy seascapes."

"You do that." Robin hugged her binder and tape measure to her chest. "Have a good day, Ethan."

His gaze seemed to caress her in a very unprofessional manner. At least he hadn't leaned toward her, or put his hands on her. She might forget all about her good intentions. "I'll see you tomorrow afternoon."

"I'll be here." She smiled to break the tension. "Now get busy and find something for me to work with."

"I'll do my best."

ETHAN CLOSED THE DOOR, then leaned against the solid wood as he let out a long, deep breath. He'd almost blown it. As he'd watched Robin walk through his rooms, he'd nearly gotten up a dozen times and taken her in his arms. He'd had no idea how seeing her in his house would affect him. He'd assumed—naively, he now realized—that he could interact with her on a professional level and not want to kiss her until all thoughts of business vanished from her head.

He pushed away from the door and walked into

the kitchen. At least she was only working on the living and dining rooms. If she'd ventured into his bedroom, he wasn't sure how he would have reacted. Followed her inside? Taken her in his arms? Asked her if she'd like to check out his king-size bed?

"Stop it," he mumbled as he opened the refrigerator and pulled out a cold can of soda. He rested the frosty metal against his forehead. Had he been a complete fool when he'd impulsively asked Robin to decorate his home? Hiring her seemed such a good idea at the time. Knowing how she longed to express her creativity, how lonely she must be in Ranger Springs, how she probably needed something to fill her days…

What had he gotten himself into?

He popped the soda cap and took a long drink. As soon as he finished mowing, he decided, he'd take a look around for something from his childhood. Maybe he'd call his mother and ask her for advice, although explaining to her that he was working with a decorator would no doubt have her rolling around laughing. She'd often commented that he'd made "bachelor chic" a permanent part of his life.

Maybe she wasn't just talking about his decorating, come to think of it.

Frowning, he walked through the living room and stared at the magazines Robin had left. Tonight he'd look through every page of them between innings of the ball game. After all, he didn't have a date. He didn't have to work. And the quicker he came up with his personal preferences, the faster Robin could get busy decorating.

He hadn't been this distracted and out of control since high school—and he really didn't like the feeling.

Chapter Seven

For the first time since moving to Ranger Springs, Robin felt excited about getting up every day. She wasn't making as much progress as she usually did with a client, but at least the company was great. Even keeping her project secret from the citizens of the small town proved to be fun and challenging.

She'd never before heard as many thinly veiled questions about who she was working for as she had in the last several days. Jimmy Mack at the hardware store guessed a different person each time he saw her, which was often, since she kept going in for paint swatches and samples of molding. Thelma and Joyce, regulars during lunch at the Four Square Café, guessed she'd been hired by the Franklins, but Gina put a stop to those speculations. One day while she stood in line to cash a small check, Robin overheard the pastor of the Methodist church ask the banker if he'd hired her to redecorate his house.

All the mystery was really quite amusing...until she heard rumors that she and Ethan were dating.

Apparently no one put two and two together and figured out *he* was her client. Or perhaps they just couldn't believe the single chief of police would want his home decorated.

If his neighbors had seen her coming and going in the late afternoon or evening, what did they think she was bringing over in her overstuffed purse and binder? Massage oil and risqué photos? And what about that stack of magazines? Did they believe Ethan needed a little encouragement from *Playboy?* She had no idea how the mind of a small-town resident worked, but Robin found the process amusing, as long as Ethan suffered no repercussions.

Over the past three days, he no longer looked at her constantly, or made remarks that could be taken more than one way. She wasn't sure if increased contact had made her less appealing to him, or if her first visit to his house had been just a fluke. Whatever the reason, she felt much more relaxed when they met to discuss a decorating strategy.

At least they'd finally decided on one: Southwestern country. Ethan had discovered an old arrowhead collection in his closet, and remembered a favorite Native American blanket from his childhood. He'd called his mother, and she'd located the piece at the family home in West. Robin was looking forward to seeing the blanket, which was to arrive in the mail today. She hoped some of the paint colors she wanted to use would compliment the vivid design so common in the woven works of art. A combination of heavy pine furniture and "homey" touches would bring life to the bland interior of the house.

Today, now that they'd chosen the basics, they were going on their first shopping excursion to see if they could find appropriate accessories. Ethan's fear of being caught shopping at an antique mall or gift store was almost comical, except that Robin could understand his misgivings. He simply didn't want to become the topic of conversation for folks in town, whether they were speculating on who he was dating or whether he was redecorating his house. As a public figure, he was automatically in the spotlight, but he also had a right to privacy.

She pulled into his driveway and parked beneath the low branches of a cottonwood tree, out of sight of the road. Ethan pushed open the back door, apparently in a hurry to be on the road.

Or in a hurry to have this task over, she thought with a smile. She knew many men viewed shopping as slow torture.

"Ready?" he asked, jingling his keys as he headed for the Bronco.

"I'm ready. Did the blanket come yet?" He opened the door for her, ever the gentleman, and she slid into the passenger seat. At least in his larger vehicle, they'd have enough room to bring home any treasures they might find.

"No, but it should be here this afternoon."

"Great. I'm looking forward to seeing it with the colors we've chosen."

Ethan walked around the Bronco, his posture a

bit more tense than usual. Robin wanted to ask him why, but she felt the inquiry would sound too personal.

"Are you sure this place in San Marcus will have something I'll like?" he asked as he slid behind the wheel.

"You can never be certain of specific inventories, but they specialize in Texas memorabilia and accessories."

"Okay," he said, sounding about as excited as if he were attending his own execution. He pulled out of his driveway onto the road.

Robin laughed. "Don't overwhelm me with your enthusiasm."

"Sorry. I'm just not good at this sort of thing."

"How do you know?" She looked around as they passed many of the businesses she'd grown accustomed to in such a short period. Ranger Springs no longer seemed so foreign, although she did miss the amenities of the big city. And the money—she definitely missed having an income.

He frowned. "I don't know. It's kind of like picking out china and stuff, isn't it?"

"Now, what do you know about picking out china patterns?" she teased.

"Not very damn much," he grumbled. "Never mind. I'll be fine."

"I have faith you'll be fine once we get there. How long will that take?"

"About a half-hour." He scowled at the road ahead. "Slump down in your seat, okay? We're about to pass Susie, and she's coming out of Joyce's beauty shop. If she sees you with me, I'm dead meat.''

Robin giggled as she hunched down as far as the seat belt would allow. "This town has you wrapped around its finger," she observed with good-natured criticism. "And I'll bet most people think you're really in charge, don't they."

"I have no idea," he said nonchalantly. "I'm just trying to avoid more gossip."

"More?"

"You can get up now. We're on the state highway, so we probably won't see anyone else who'll be able to recognize you."

"Seriously, have you been the subject of a lot of gossip?"

He paused before answering the question. "I don't know. Not a lot, but there was a time… Let's just say that the people of this town took an interest in my personal life a few years ago and haven't let go since."

"Will you tell me why?"

He shook his head. "Not yet."

Robin pursed her lips and settled back into the seat. Another facet to Ethan's character she had yet to uncover. She'd thought she'd created a pretty comprehensive inventory of his traits the other night, but obviously her list wasn't complete. He had secrets he wanted to hide from *her.* Apparently everyone else in town knew the story.

Of course, he had said "not yet" instead of shutting her out completely. Maybe he was planning on revealing more to her later. Robin decided to wait for Ethan to tell her.

They traveled in silence for several miles. Robin enjoyed watching the countryside pass by quickly. This drive wasn't as scenic as the one they'd taken to the German restaurant the other night, but she enjoyed seeing the rock-strewn hills, occasional cattle and ever-present, scrubby cactus that grew alongside tall prairie grasses and scattered clumps of red and yellow wildflowers.

Soon they neared San Marcus, a picturesque college town that also boasted Aquarena Springs. When she was younger, she remembered, she'd seen travel brochures featuring Ralph, the diving pig. She'd always wanted to see Ralph, but her parents hadn't considered a trip from Houston to San Marcus a top priority. Later, Great-aunt Sylvia had explained that there wasn't just one Ralph, but a series of piglets who dived into the clear springs to cheering audiences. She'd said Robin could go later because there would always be a new Ralph, but Robin wondered if that was true.

She was going to ask Ethan about Ralph, but he looked even more grim as they approached I-35. The antique mall was located on the service road, not far away.

She wanted to place her hand on his arm, to comfort him, but his expression kept her from acting on her instincts. She settled on verbal reassurances. "Ethan, I hope we can enjoy ourselves."

He looked doubtful. "Don't worry about it. I'll be fine. Just don't expect a lot of input from me."

"You need to tell me what you like."

"Hey, I'm the guy with the boring beige sofa and white walls, remember? Doesn't that tell you something about my taste?"

"No, not really." She watched as he maneuvered into the parking lot. "You didn't have many options before."

"What makes you think I would have chosen something different if I did have other choices?"

She frowned as she considered his question. Why was he putting himself down? She'd seen far more atrocious furnishings than his rather bland living and dining rooms. "I think you're just nervous about shopping."

He turned the key, shutting off the engine. "I'm not nervous. I'm just not good at this sort of thing."

"So you've already claimed. And I'd just like to say that you've never been shopping with me."

"You may be real disappointed." He unbuckled his seat belt and opened his door.

"With you? I doubt it." But he was already walking around toward the passenger side.

"Don't say you weren't forewarned," he said as he opened her door. "I'm not exactly Mr. Excitement, you know."

She slipped down from the seat and met his tense gaze. "You're kidding, right?"

"I wish I were." He frowned, forestalling her

comments as he urged her toward the entrance. "Let's go shopping."

"I think I'd rather talk about you."

"No such luck," he said with finality. He opened the glass door. "Come on. Let's go find some accessories I'll love."

Robin shook her head and frowned. Ethan was in a strange mood today, but at least she'd gotten him to the antique mall. With a little luck, they'd find some great items. With a little skill, she hoped to talk him out of his dark mood before it was time to return to Ranger Springs.

"WHAT DO YOU THINK OF THIS?" Robin asked, holding up a framed Texas flag about the size of a diploma.

"The frame looks a little beat-up," Ethan said, eyeing the aged wood skeptically. The poor thing looked like it had been stored in someone's toolshed for about two decades.

Robin laughed. "It's supposed to look that way. It's called 'distressing.' The wood is sometimes old, like off a barn or fence, but sometimes new wood is chemically treated, scarred, hammered or just soaked in water and lye to make it appear aged."

Ethan shook his head. "Whatever. You're the decorator." Actually, he found this whole shopping experience "distressing." Robin chatted away, placed her hand on his arm when she wanted his attention, and even grabbed him occasionally when she found something that excited her.

Maybe he should have gone shopping with women before. He hadn't realized someone else's old stuff could be so exciting. Then again, he'd be competing for attention against metal trays, cut-glass candy dishes and old wood frames. The idea that women found those items more exhilarating than a flesh-and-blood man was a little disheartening.

Hell, it was a lot disheartening. He'd meant what he'd said earlier to Robin; he wasn't particularly interesting or exciting to women. At least, that was the impression he'd gotten from women in the past—two particular women. They used words like "stable" and "solid" to describe him. In his book, those terms meant he didn't set their hearts aflutter.

Maybe when he'd been an FBI agent, just because of the perceived danger of the occupation. But a small-town cop? No way had that improved his image as dating material. Or as marriage material—not that he was looking. The phrase "Been there, done that" applied doubly in his case.

"Ethan, I want you to approve of the purchases. After all, this is your house."

"I know, but like I told you before, I'm not good at this decorating stuff. Give me a target range or a city council meeting, and I'm fine. Put me in an antique mall, and I'm like a duck out of water."

"I understand," she said with a sigh. "Just promise me you'll let me know if you really don't like something I've picked out."

"I promise." He reached out and snagged the

framed Lone Star flag. "I'll hold on to this for you."

"Okay." She turned her attention back to the row of booths, each rented by a different person. The proprietors seemed to specialize in different items. One might have lots of toys, while another had china plates and teacups.

His eyes settled on a booth at the end. "I'm going to wander down there," he told Robin.

She nodded, caught up in assessing an old pickle crock.

A few minutes later, she joined him. "What did you find?"

"I'm not sure this would work, but I kind of like these old license plates." He turned and smiled. "Kind of ties in with my law enforcement career."

"Oh, I see. Patrolling the streets and all that."

"And locking the bad guys up so they can turn out these babies in prison."

Robin laughed. "An excellent choice. Which ones did you like?"

A few minutes later, she had an armful of the somewhat rusty, sometimes bent plates. He was about to take them from her, when one of the ladies he'd seen up front joined them in the aisle.

"Can I put those at the counter for you?" she asked with a friendly smile.

"Yes, thank you," Robin replied. "We still have a lot of shopping to do."

Ethan shook his head, rolling his eyes a bit to tease her.

The clerk laughed. "Husbands are always like that. They never want to shop, but they're always ready to complain when we spend their money."

Ethan opened his mouth to tell the woman he and Robin weren't married, but she'd already turned and walked away.

"A common assumption," Robin explained.

"Not for me," he said, wondering just how much like a couple they appeared. He'd tried damn hard to make sure no one in Ranger Springs matched him up with a single woman. Even when he went to statewide meetings, he acted polite but professional around the women in law enforcement. He didn't want anyone to get the wrong idea. One simple shopping trip, and this lady had him married to Robin Cummings.

He took a deep breath, then exhaled, pushing the image out of his mind. What a disaster they'd be together, with her fancy, city ways and his low-key, small-town life-style. He'd be surprised if she lasted the two months of her agreement, much less a lifetime.

No, women like Robin weren't for him, at least in the long run. If he'd met her while he was in Houston, and she wasn't connected through their aunts, then maybe...yes, definitely, he would have pursued her. Spent some good times with her. Maybe had a hot and passionate short-term affair.

But not like this. Not in his town, with many eyes on them. He couldn't risk the concern people would show. He didn't want to endure their sympathy when Robin left town with a chunk of his heart.

"Ethan?"

He turned his attention back to Robin, who was frowning at him.

"What's wrong? You looked like you were a million miles away."

"I'm fine," he said, guiding her out of the booth and back into the aisle. Her arm felt warm and firm beneath his fingers, her skin so incredibly soft that he had a hard time keeping his mind on the task at hand. "Let's finish shopping. I'm about ready for lunch."

"They have a tearoom here at the antique mall."

Ethan made a rude noise, then softened his opinion with a smile. "How about some real food? Barbecue? Tex-Mex?"

Robin laughed. "I should have remembered who I was with. No sissy food for you, right?"

"Damn straight, woman," he said in a cross between a drawl and a growl.

Robin laughed, then stopped. "Seriously, Ethan, you're doing great. I know how much men hate to shop, especially at places like this."

Again, he was amazed by the warmth he felt when she touched him, or when he touched her. And her smell, so clean and lightly floral, drifted across the heated air separating them.

"I'm trying my best," he said, looking down into the depths of her brown eyes. *I'm trying my best to keep my hands off you, and to remember we didn't meet in Houston and we aren't going to have a short but hot fling.*

Just then a big burly guy, wearing low slung jeans and a tan work shirt, looking as though he might drive an eighteen-wheeler or a tow truck, plowed down the aisle. As he passed, he scratched his whiskers with one hand as he clutched a delicate porcelain figurine in the other.

"Well, maybe *some* men like to shop," Robin whispered, breaking the mood with her quip.

Ethan chuckled. "If that's what it takes, I'll try to be more of the sensitive modern male."

Robin smiled. "I like you just fine the way you are."

His heart beat a little faster as he walked beside her, but he didn't dare say anything.

"For a client, you're okay," she added. He realized that once again he'd allowed his libido to outdistance his brain. He really had to get his thoughts and desires under control, or this decorating project was going to turn into a real pain in the...neck.

On Monday after the shopping trip, Robin paused before knocking on Ethan's door to adjust her royal-blue, sleeveless cotton sweater over the waistband of off-white pleated shorts. When she called on a client in Houston or the suburbs, she wore simple, stylish dresses, or slacks and tops. Since there was nothing hotter on the face of this planet than panty hose worn during a Texas summer, a wardrobe of shorts and sandals while working was an enormous bonus.

He finally opened the door after she'd knocked twice. Instead of the coolly composed Ethan she'd come to expect, he appeared frazzled. His dark hair looked as if he'd run his fingers through it again and again. His shirt wasn't fully buttoned, exposing more of his broad chest than she'd seen before. A nice view, but she had to wonder what was wrong.

"Is this a bad time?" she asked, as he pulled the door wide.

"No, it's not. I've just been on the phone since I got home. I hardly had time to change." He looked down at his partially open shirt, then quickly fastened the two errant buttons. "Sorry. I guess I really didn't have enough time to change."

"It's okay," she said, stepping inside. She felt sympathy for anyone who was having a bad day, because she'd been there often enough herself. In the past three weeks, she'd made a major decision about her future, re-evaluated her relationships and decided to start over. She placed her hand on his bare forearm. "I can come back at another time if you'd like."

He looked down at her hand, pale against his darker tan. Her nails, kept fairly short because of her work, rested against some very impressive muscle. The gesture had been instinctive, something she would do to any friend, but suddenly she felt as though she'd crossed an invisible barrier. He must have felt it, too, because he slowly pulled his arm away.

When she looked into his eyes, she saw heat that had nothing to do with the Texas summer. His cheeks appeared a bit flushed, and he held himself so very still that the two of them seemed momentarily frozen in time. She heard the sounds of the afternoon—a car slowly traveling down the road in front of his house, birds chirping all around them, a lawn mower buzzing in the distance—but she couldn't have moved if her life depended on it.

Seconds later, he took a deep breath and broke the spell. She let her hand fall to her side as she felt a blush creep down her neck from her own hot cheeks. "I didn't mean—"

"It's okay." He stepped back, giving her even more space. "Come on in. Let's get started."

"Ethan, are you sure?"

"Positive." He sounded impatient, almost angry. "I made enough dinner for two. If you haven't eaten, you're welcome to join me."

She resisted saying "Are you sure?" again. Instead, she opted for a more professional tone. Something to diffuse the unexpected tension at the doorway just now. "That would be lovely."

Since she was so familiar with the house by now, she walked into the breakfast area and placed her materials on the table. Ethan followed with an opened box he picked up from the coffee table.

"Is that the blanket?" she asked, when he placed it beside her things on the table.

"Yes. It's a bit smaller than I remember, but I still like the colors." He pulled the blanket from the plastic bag his mother had obviously used to store it for many years. "We bought this in Arizona when we went on vacation one summer. I must have been eight or nine. I remember my dad saying we had too much stuff in the car already, but my mother just kept negotiating with the owner of the shop."

Ethan stopped to stroke the thick weaving. "In the end, my dad gave in, although he put on a show of grumbling. My mother usually got her way," Ethan added with a smile.

"They must have been very close."

"Yes, they were. Still are," he said, shaking off the memories. "Happily retired in West. I'm just glad they didn't decide to throw away all my old stuff. I'd almost forgotten about this blanket until you started insisting I must have *something* personal."

"Most people have things of importance, but over the years they get pushed back in drawers or tops of closets and temporarily forgotten. It's nice to bring them out and use them in the decor."

"If you say so." He shook his head and grinned ruefully. "If I tried this on my own, I'm afraid it would look like I stuck an old blanket on the wall."

Robin laughed. "I'll make sure the whole room looks good together. After all, that's why you're paying me the big bucks."

Ethan looked surprised for a moment, then realized she was teasing. They'd already agreed upon a fee, which she'd kept at a minimum because of the "fringe benefits" of working with the sexy police chief. Not that she was going to acknowledge the attraction she felt any more than he was going to take any action to change their status.

He chuckled, but Robin felt his mind still wasn't one-hundred percent involved in the decorating project, or even in their conversation. He must have had a bad day, but since his job was so often confidential, she didn't feel comfortable asking.

Besides, saying the equivalent of "Honey, how was your day?" seemed way too intimate for two friendly acquaintances. Or a client and a professional.

Robin pushed the decorating materials and blanket aside, while Ethan finished preparations on the dinner. Within a few minutes, she had glasses of iced tea on his mint-green place mats, and he'd deposited a bowl of chicken and dumplings in the middle of the oak table. After adding a green salad for each of them, he took his seat.

"Is this one of Aunt Bess's frozen meals?"

"No, I made this one myself yesterday afternoon. Every now and then, I decide to cook."

"I'm impressed," she said, as the steam wafted toward her. "Smells delicious."

He looked at her sideways, a fork full of lettuce and cucumber poised near his mouth. "Surprised I didn't scorch it?"

The obvious reference to her own disastrous

"cooking" made her lift her eyebrows. "Not really. I know lots of men who can cook."

"How about your ex-fiancé? Did he know his way around the kitchen?"

Surprised by the question, Robin paused before attacking her salad. "No, he didn't. The only time he went into the kitchen was to get a beer out of the refrigerator or to add ice to his glass."

"Hmm." Ethan devoted his attention to his food.

"Not that he was a big drinker. Just socially. He simply wasn't handy in the kitchen."

"I suppose you two were planning on eating out a lot."

"Well, yes, I suppose we were." She wondered why Ethan was asking these questions, making these comments. He was in an strange mood tonight—different than on Saturday, but still more moody than usual—and she wished she understood why. "Is that so odd?"

"Not in a big city like Houston, I suppose. Here in a small town, yeah, it's pretty odd."

"Well, we didn't live in a small town," she said, getting irritated with his comments. "We were planning on living in his town house for several years. Perhaps moving into a larger house later." *If* they'd decided to have children, which they'd never seriously discussed. She put her fork beside her plate. "Why are you making our lives sound like something…unnatural?"

He pushed away from the table, then carried his bowl of half-eaten salad into the kitchen. She watched him run his fingers through his hair again, leaving it even more disheveled.

"I'm sorry. I'm not trying to pick a fight. I've just had a long day, and then I saw you..." He walked back to the table, took a seat and dished out the chicken and dumplings. "I shouldn't take my bad mood out on you."

"I agree with you. If you didn't want to meet tonight, you could have said so."

"I want to get this decorating project started. Heck, I want to get it finished."

Robin began to understand. Ethan's world was being disrupted. He was acting out, as many people did when they were in the midst of an upheaval. And as his decorator, she was the cause because she forced them to make decisions, then had their carpets ripped out, their walls painted, their cabinets stripped. "I understand. Decorating sounds like such a pleasant little diversion, but then reality sets in."

He looked at her intently across the short distance. Steam seemed to rise from him as well as from the bowl between them. "You're right. Reality has set in. I'll try to keep things in perspective."

"And I'll try to keep your life from being too disrupted."

Ethan nodded—even though Robin was already proving a disruption to his well ordered life.

IF ETHAN DIDN'T GET AWAY from her soon, he was going to do something he'd regret. He'd made it through dinner with her tonight. He'd survived the shopping trip to the antique mall, where they'd been mistaken for a married couple. For the past two days, he'd sat beside her on the couch and looked at magazines, swatches of fabric, chips of paint and various other decorative touches she thought might be good for his house.

But what was good for his house, he'd soon discovered, was killing him.

"I'll arch the iron stars above the framed flag, then use the rest to anchor the corners of the blanket," Robin said, laying out the rusty metal pieces on the coffee table. "How does that sound?"

"Fine." He shifted on the cushions, wondering how long he'd have to sit here tonight and endure her soft fragrance and sexy voice.

"Now all we have to do is decide on the wall color." She started sorting through the paint samples, bending over the coffee table. Her sleek, golden hair slid forward along her jaw, making his fingers itch to touch it.

He had to admit this truth: he couldn't be around Robin without wanting her. Oh, he'd tried. He'd told himself a hundred times that she was a family friend. A newcomer in town. A lonely, recently unattached young woman in a strange place. There were a dozen reasons why he absolutely couldn't become involved with Robin Cummings.

And then there was the issue of the ex-fiancé. When Ethan had first met Robin, he'd felt sorry for the jilted guy. Hell, he'd identified with him! Now all he could think about was some other guy spending his days—and nights—with Robin. The more he thought about it, the more angry he became. He knew his feelings were irrational. Dammit, the whole relationship with her was crazy! They were as mismatched as fine crystal and jelly jar glasses.

Unfortunately, his body wasn't listening to all the reasons he couldn't get involved with Robin. If he sat beside her for another five minutes, smelling her light perfume, listening to her soft, intelligent voice, he was going to take her by the shoulders and seal his lips over hers. To hell with good intentions, small town life, family connections and employer responsibilities. To hell with being chief of police.

"Ethan, what's wrong?"

His eyes jerked open as he felt her put her soft but strong hand on his forearm, just as she'd done earlier this evening when he'd been in such a crabby mood. Lord, she was driving him crazy! He shook his head as he jumped up from the sofa.

"I've got to go," he said, hoping she didn't hear the panic in his voice. He walked to the mantel and reached inside the flowery little ceramic jar Aunt Bess kept there. Success and freedom! "Here's a key. Feel free to look around all you'd like. Measure, match, do whatever you need to do. I trust your judgment. I need to…"

"What?"

He couldn't lie to her, so he simply didn't tell

her the truth. "I just need to go somewhere. I'll talk to you later."

"Ethan!"

"Sorry, Robin. I've got to go."

He glanced at her briefly, just long enough to see the shocked and worried expression on her pretty face. Dammit, he didn't want to do this to her. But more important, he didn't want to reveal his true feelings. She'd already let him know she wasn't ready for a romantic relationship, and he could certainly understand her position. She wanted to be friends. She was working for him. He couldn't abuse her trust by showing how much he wanted her.

He let himself out, then shut the door as quietly as possible. There was only one place to go at a time like this. He needed a testosterone-rich environment—one without any female distractions. A place where no one would ask him what color was his favorite, what style he preferred or what he thought about every tiny detail.

Chapter Eight

"Oh, God, I've done it again," Robin whispered. This time not with family or a lover, but with a client. She'd been so certain she could keep her relationship with Ethan professional. She'd reveled in the opportunity to spend time with him without the uncomfortable attraction that had sizzled between them at first. Never in a million years had she suspected that she'd push him away.

Robin sat on the couch long after Ethan had hurried out the front door. She'd sat in the quiet house and listened to him start the engine of his Bronco, then back out of the driveway. The tires hadn't actually squealed when he drove away, but close.

He couldn't wait to get away from her. He couldn't stand to be in the same room with her. In the same house with her. She felt so stunned, so confused, that she sank down onto the sofa. She doubted her legs would support her another minute.

She hadn't felt this way in weeks, not since... Gig.

Her head snapped up. Could she compare the two

men? Certainly not in most regards. She and Gig had known each other socially for years. They'd been a couple for months and months. She'd known him as an easygoing and charming man, living up to his heritage and upbringing in one of Houston's "good" families.

Toward the end, when they—mostly *she*—were planning the wedding, the honeymoon and the move to his town house, everything had changed. Several scenes with her ex-fiancé flashed unbidden and unwelcome in her mind. Angry, upsetting confrontations in which he'd claimed she was smothering him. Mean, heartless accusations that he needed time apart from her.

Just like Ethan, tonight, when he'd rushed out of his own home.

Had she ruined a relationship she'd begun to treasure? Had she irrevocably crossed the line from friendly to personal, from concerned to smothering?

Burying her face in her hands, Robin let humiliation wash over her. She was an adult, not some needy child, but she'd acted like one—again. Sitting on the sofa in the house of a man she'd known less than two weeks, she felt so alone. She wanted to be back in Houston, where she could run to her Great-aunt Sylvia the way she had so many times before. She wanted to curl up on the fancy brocade love seat, hug a cushy velvet pillow, and wait for the tea and cookies her great-aunt served for all types of emotional crises.

But she wasn't in Houston. She was in Ranger

Springs, all grown up…in theory. Great-aunt Sylvia was a couple of hundred miles away, blissfully unaware that her great-niece was reverting to her childish need for someone to love.

Not that she was in love with Ethan, Robin reminded herself. Nothing of the sort. He was just her only friend in town at the moment. As her only friend—and a client, to boot—Ethan had become the person she'd focused on. They'd shared meals, laughs and conversations about their likes and dislikes. She'd needed his opinion on this decorating project, so they'd spent hours together this past week.

It wasn't that she'd had to convince herself their time together was necessary; the idea that she'd been leaning on him hadn't entered her mind.

Had she permanently destroyed their working relationship? She sincerely hoped not. She needed to finish this job. She needed to keep Ethan's friendship. And the only way to have both was to apologize and explain—no matter how painful that might be.

SCHULTZ'S ROADHOUSE wasn't too crowded when Ethan stepped inside the smoky interior. This wasn't one of his favorite places, but it was just what he needed tonight.

Most of the patrons were pretty harmless, but occasionally a drifter or temporary laborer had too much to drink and caused a ruckus. Ethan had arrested his share of drunks, DWIs, and disorderly conducts here.

The regulars at the bar turned to look at him, nodded a greeting, then went back to their drinks. A few men at one of the tables smiled and motioned him over, but he shook his head. He remembered meeting them at the feed store, but he wasn't in any mood for company.

No, all he wanted to do was nurse a beer while his blood cooled. Maybe watch a sports update on ESPN. Maybe forget he'd left Robin sitting alone in his house.

He walked to the end of the bar and pulled out a stool. "Give me a light draft, Olive," he said to the weathered, experienced bartender. She'd worked at Schultz's for longer than he'd been in town.

He didn't want to make conversation or deal with any drunks tonight. He'd used up every ounce of self-control and congeniality this past week by being around Robin way too much for his peace of mind.

"Here you go, Chief," Olive said, placing a frosty mug in front of him. "Heard you might be going out with that cute young lady from Houston."

He took a sip of beer. "Nope."

Olive shrugged. "Guess I heard wrong."

Ethan ignored the attempt to get a gossip update. All he wanted to do was scowl into his beer and ignore his troubles. He had a feeling Robin wasn't going away anytime soon, which meant she'd be asking more questions, digging for more opinions, as soon as she found him again. But she wasn't going to find him here. For a while at least, he'd be safe.

"You just look like a man with woman trouble."

Ethan shook his head and chuckled into his beer. "I thought I'd put all those troubles behind me, Olive."

"You know what they say, Chief. Third time's a charm."

"CHIEF, THERE'S SOMEONE here to see you," Susie said over the intercom.

"Who is it?"

"Robin Cummings," his dispatcher and receptionist said in a tone that sounded just a bit smug. Just a bit too inquisitive. Had she noticed Robin in his car on Saturday when they'd driven to San Marcus?

Dammit, he wasn't ready to face Robin after the way he'd acted last night. He still hadn't decided what he was going to tell her about his behavior. Not that he needed to come up with an excuse. He wanted to be honest, but he wasn't sure Robin was ready or willing to listen to the truth.

"Chief, can I send her back?"

"Sure, Susie."

Ethan braced himself to face Robin. He straightened the collar of his uniform shirt, smoothed back his already tidy hair and sat up straighter in his office chair. Then, before he could think of anything to say, she walked into his corner office.

The morning sun caught her in a soft, fuzzy shaft of light. She looked beautiful, but also vulnerable. Had his desertion last night hurt her so much?

"Hello, Robin," he said as he rose from his office chair and walked around the desk. "How are you?"

"Fine." She looked up at him, her expression clouded. "How are *you?*"

"I'm okay. A little embarrassed by my behavior last night." He motioned for her to have a seat in one of the three leather-and-wood chairs facing his desk, then he sat down beside her.

"Really? Me, too."

"You? I'm the one who acted like an ass."

"With reason, I'm positive."

"I'm not sure there's ever a good reason for being rude."

"I didn't think you were rude. I knew you had your reasons." She smiled slightly. "I didn't understand what they were at the time, but I was certain something was wrong."

"You're giving me too much credit. The fault was mine."

"No, I don't think so. I—"

"Chief, I need your signature on this transfer—" Rick Alvarado, one of Ethan's officers, walked into the office without looking up. When he did, he stopped and stared. "Sorry. I didn't realize you had a visitor."

"That's okay." Ethan stood up. "Let's see what you have."

He paged through the forms that he'd been expecting from another jurisdiction, then signed his name. "Here you go, Alvarado."

Rick jerked his too-appreciative gaze away from Robin. "Thanks, Chief." He looked back at Robin and nodded. "Ma'am."

"Miss, actually," she said with a smile.

"You're new in town, aren't you?" Rick asked.

"Yes, I am." She offered her hand. "Robin Cummings."

"Pleased to meet you. I'm—"

"Late for patrol duty," Ethan injected. Didn't Alvarado have something better to do than hang around and act like a blabbering idiot? You'd think the guy had never seen a young, attractive woman before!

"Nice to meet you," he said on the way out.

"Same here," Robin replied. She turned to Ethan as soon as the hallway was clear. "You're testy today."

"I sure am. Must have something to do with last night."

"Oh," she said. "About last night—"

"Not here," he said. "It's nearly lunchtime. Let's go someplace where we can talk without interruptions."

She glanced around the brightly lit office, hesitated just a moment, and answered, "All right."

They made it halfway down the hall before Susie found them. "Chief, are you leaving?"

"Right. Lunch." He tried to steer Robin out the door before anyone asked any more questions, but from the curious look on his dispatcher's face, he wasn't going to get his wish.

"You're the interior decorator from Houston, aren't you?"

"Yes, I am. Robin Cummings."

"I'm Susie O'Donald. I just love decorating. I tape my favorite shows that are on during the day, and play them back over the weekend. I have this older house, and I practice the painting techniques. One room is sponged, one is stenciled and I'm working on a striate effect for the wainscoting in my entryway."

"Susie, don't you have to get back to the phones?"

"In a minute, Chief Parker. Rick is covering for me while I take a little break."

"We need to go," Ethan said, impatient to get away before anyone else discovered him with Robin. No telling what kind of stories about him would be circulating tomorrow.

Probably something close to the truth.

"Where did you have in mind?" Robin asked, as he took her elbow. He led her down the hallway at as brisk a pace as possible without making her run to keep up.

"There's a beautiful spot you should see while

you're here in town. You probably don't have any scenery like it back in Houston.''

"I'm sure we don't." She paused as they exited the rear door to the municipal building. ''Are you going to drag me on foot to this special place?''

Ethan let go of her elbow and ran a hand through his hair. "Sorry. I just wanted to get out of there before someone else interrupted us.''

"Before someone else saw me, you mean.''

"I'm not ashamed to be seen with you.''

"But you don't want to explain my presence to anyone else.''

He nodded. "I keep my private life private.''

"I understand. I didn't mean to put you in an uncomfortable position.''

He looked at her in the sunlight, her hair, touched by gold highlights, dancing in the breeze. She looked lovely. Slightly defiant, proud, but also vulnerable. She'd never looked more appealing.

Maybe being alone with her wasn't such a good idea.

"It's not your fault.''

She turned her head to the side. ''Are we talking about last night—or being seen with me inside your offices?''

ROBIN STOPPED and eyed the cruiser with skepticism. "I'm not sure I want to get away that badly.'' She'd never been in a police car before, and she was fairly certain she could forgo the experience now.

"I need to take the car because I'm on duty. If something comes up, I'll have to respond."

"Then maybe we should talk later." The concept of being in danger with the chief of police wasn't on her agenda for this interlude in a small town. If she wanted to live dangerously, she'd drive alone in certain parts of Houston in her parents' Mercedes.

"I don't plan on chasing any bad guys or speeders," he said as he opened the door for her. "But if I do get a call, I promise I'll let you turn on the lights and siren."

"Gee, thanks," she said as she slid into the passenger side. Before he had walked around the car, she'd fastened her seat belt. As Ethan started the engine, she looked around the inside of the vehicle. There were enough gadgets, gauges and gizmos to pilot the space shuttle.

"Not what you expected in a small-town cop car, is it."

"Not exactly." Robin chuckled as she shook her head. "Not that I've given the interior design of police vehicles much thought."

They pulled out onto the main road, which intersected both the state highway and the town square. Robin was surprised that Ethan drove toward town, since the place he wanted to show her was scenic—which to her meant rural. But she didn't say anything as they drove by the hardware store where she'd spent so much time lately, or the pharmacy with its old-fashioned soda fountain, or the Four Square Café where she'd eaten lunch several times this past week. They drove past older houses, then passed another intersection where a farm-to-market road angled off to parts unknown. Soon the terrain changed from nearly flat to rolling hills. Pastures replaced front yards, and scrubby mesquite trees took the place of live oaks. Ethan turned off the narrow road onto a gravel path that wound through the hills.

They slowly descended the trail as the midday sun beat down on the hood of the patrol car. Ethan took a sharp left into a stand of weeping willows and cottonwoods. Edging the car completely into the shade, he rolled down the windows, then turned off the engine. Man-made sounds were replaced by the buzz of insects, the rustle of leaves and the murmur of running water.

"Is there a stream nearby?"

"Yes, just below the bank. The scenery is great. Would you care to walk down there?"

"Sure." She didn't wait for him to walk around and open the passenger door. Ethan reminded her of the gallant sort of gentleman she'd rarely encountered in real life, but had fantasized about when she was younger and more idealistic. If she wasn't careful, she'd mistake his natural inclinations for something more private. She'd confuse their professional relationship for a personal one, and she couldn't allow herself that folly.

"Your purse is safe here," he said. "No one else

is around, and I can hear the gravel if another car approaches.''

"Okay, lead the way.''

She followed him across solid ground liberally dotted with wildflowers and wild grasses. The dappled sunlight skipped across the dark earth as the willows and lanky cottonwoods swayed in the breeze. A moment later, Ethan pulled aside a curtain of willow branches, and Robin stepped through...into another beautiful world.

A shallow stream ran over a bed of gray-and-brown rocks, some of them jutting out of the water and along the banks. Hills sloped down, covered with red, yellow and white wildflowers. Across the stream, a small, quaint stone house sat abandoned, its walls twined with flowering vines.

Robin wandered toward the water, picking out a flat-top rock to settle upon. Ethan followed, standing over her. She didn't look up, but she saw his shadow on the uneven stones and tufts of grass near the streambed.

"Thank you for bringing me here. It's beautiful.''

"I thought you'd like it, since you have a good sense of color and...things.''

Robin smiled. "Balance and harmony. This place has a wonderful sense of calmness that we can only try to achieve inside our homes.''

"About that design business.'' Ethan settled on another rock, one that didn't look all that comfortable. "I really do want you to finish decorating my house. I just got a little crazy last night."

"I think I know why, too."

"You do?" He sounded surprised. Maybe a little shocked.

Robin nodded. "That's why I came to talk to you. After you left, I tried to understand what had happened. If I'd heard your phone ring, or your police radio call, I would have assumed you were needed for some emergency. But you were just sitting there—then you said you had to leave."

"I know, and I'm sorry. I felt really bad about leaving you alone. My behavior was inexcusable, but I would like to try to explain."

"I think I need to tell you what I realized after you left, if you don't mind."

Ethan squinted at her through the bright sunlight. "Whatever you'd like. Although I think the fault is entirely my own."

Robin shook her head. "This goes back to my wedding. Or to be more accurate, why I didn't have a wedding."

Ethan frowned. "I don't understand."

"Please, let me tell you about why Gig and I broke up." Robin looked across the peaceful stream, clearing her mind of the feelings Ethan stirred in her. He'd wanted to talk about last night, but she needed to go back farther. Back into her childhood.

Chapter Nine

"I suppose I was always one of those clingy children. You've seen them in the stores. They hang off their mothers like living accessories. The difference is that my parents wouldn't tolerate such behavior. I learned to be a well-behaved daughter. Instead of showing *them* affection, I had Great-aunt Sylvia. She didn't have children of her own, but she would have made a wonderful mother. She held me, read to me, had tea parties for me and my dolls. We were the best of friends for as long as I remember, until I went off to college." Robin smiled sadly at the memories. "When I came back home, I suppose I was just a little too big to curl up in her lap."

"But you still wanted to."

"Yes, at times." She sighed. "I'd known Gig for most of my life. He was two years older and had already established himself in his career at his father's bank."

"I know this is way off the subject, but where did he get a name like Gig?"

Robin chuckled. "Family tradition. Like his father and his grandfather, he graduated from Texas A&M. So he took the nickname from the 'gig 'em Aggies' saying when he was a kid."

"I suppose it's a better name than Biff or Chip," Ethan quipped, obviously not impressed by the sometimes silly nicknames her social set chose.

Robin nodded. "I suppose I just accepted it at the time, although looking back on it, the name does sound silly." She laughed as she gazed out over the water. "I'm having a hard time imagining a sixty-year-old Gig."

"For what it's worth, I'm glad you didn't marry a guy named after a football team."

She turned to smile at Ethan. "You know—I am, too." *For more than one reason.*

"I got you off the subject."

Robin sobered as she turned back to the peaceful setting before them. "Gig and I were thrown together at many family and social events. It seemed logical, almost inevitable, that we'd get engaged." She shrugged, remembering all the times people had said they made such a lovely couple. "So we did."

"Did you love him?"

She watched the sunlight play off the current, reminding her of the large emerald-cut diamond in the engagement ring she'd returned on her last day in Houston. And the confusion and anger in Gig's eyes as she'd told him the wedding was off. She hadn't wanted to hurt him or her family, but she finally had to admit she couldn't spend the rest of her life with him.

"I wanted to. I tried. I thought I did. Looking back, no, I didn't. I realized after I moved into the Franklin home that I loved the *idea* of being a couple far more than I loved the actual man."

"Then you made the right decision." He said the words to be encouraging, she knew, but his tone told her something else. Something she wanted to know, as soon as she'd unburdened herself and apologized once more.

"Having realized my feelings for Gig weren't the kind poets describe, I tried to understand why I felt so bad about calling off the wedding. I finally understood that most of my remorse was over my own behavior."

"What do you mean?"

"I had to admit to myself that I'd smothered him. I'd planned our evenings to be together. I'd arranged my schedule to be a part of his life. I constantly asked him about the future—what he wanted to do next year, five years, even twenty years away. Before we were married, I was mentally planning our retirement years." And yet they hadn't discussed some of the things most couples who were deeply in love considered—such as having children. Perhaps that was because deep down inside, neither one of them could make a permanent commitment. But she'd probably never know how Gig had really felt.

She sighed. "I wanted so much for the two of us

to become a family that I overwhelmed him. Gig wanted a nice, comfortable, nonpassionate marriage. Oh, not a marriage of convenience or anything like that. He wasn't a monk.''

"I don't think I need to hear this part."

"Oh." She looked up and realized she was doing it again—telling intimate details. Revealing herself to someone who didn't want to know. "Sorry. Of course you don't. Well, anyway, it turned out that Gig and I wanted far different things from a marriage. Just before I broke the engagement, he accused me of smothering him, and I know now that's exactly what I was doing.''

"No one could blame you for wanting it all. If I were to— Let's just say that my views on marriage are more in line with yours than ol' Gig's."

Robin smiled and turned to look at Ethan. "Thanks, but I know I went overboard with time spent together, planning, all the things that drove him to distraction. If I'd truly loved him, I would have noticed how he wasn't participating in the conversations, the plans. But I was so caught up in the moment that I never thought about him.'' Poor Gig. He'd probably assumed her overwhelming actions had more to do with the wedding plans than what she'd wanted—no, needed—in a relationship.

She took a long breath. "And I did the same thing with you.''

"What?''

"I got so involved with the idea of decorating your home, spending time with you in the evenings and learning about small-town life that I didn't consider your feelings. You were trying to be polite, I know." She held up her hand when he started to protest. "And you succeeded. You were so nice, so welcoming, that I let my need to belong get entirely out of hand."

"Robin, I don't think that's what happened."

"No, it's true. I know myself now, Ethan. I know how overwhelming I can be when I'm focused on one thing. I was so intent on doing a good job with your house that I drove you right out the front door!"

"That's not what happened."

"You're just being polite again."

"No, I'm not. You were honest with me. It's time I did the same."

ETHAN HADN'T DISCUSSED his personal life with anyone in the past four years. He had no need to wallow in the details; everyone in town already knew the story.

Everyone except Robin, apparently.

He supposed he should feel grateful a town that thrived on knowing everyone's business thought enough of him not to gossip about his failings. After all, they'd been witness to the last disaster, and they'd heard about the first one from family and friends who'd been on hand.

He sighed, then ran a hand through his hair. Unable to sit on the rock any longer, he picked up a handful of pebbles and walked to the edge of the creek.

"I told you about being an FBI agent in Dallas. What I didn't mention was that I was engaged when I made the decision to leave the Bureau, go back to my small-town roots." He zinged a pebble across the water, watching it skip three times before disappearing. "My fiancée, Monica, was beautiful, intelligent and very career-minded. Suffice it to say, she wasn't thrilled with the idea."

"Did she refuse to go with you?"

"Not exactly. She tried to talk me out of it. When that didn't work, she pouted for a while. Then she looked into job opportunities in Austin, San Marcus and San Antonio. We talked about her commuting. We talked about having kids someday, and how I wanted them to have the same kind of stable family life I did as a child." Ethan shrugged. "I thought everything was settled. I thought she had come around to my way of thinking."

"But she hadn't," Robin guessed.

"Not even close." Having Monica "come around to his way of thinking" had seemed logical and important four years ago. Now the words sounded…selfish. Still, she should have talked to him about her doubts. She didn't have to humiliate him before his friends and family.

He skipped another pebble across the water, this time more forcefully, as he remembered what would have been his wedding day. "She didn't call off the engagement, though. She simply left me standing at the church, looking out at all our guests and wondering what the hell had happened.''

''You didn't have a clue?''

''No! I was frantic. I thought she'd been in an accident. Or kidnapped. Or anything but the truth.''

''Which was that she couldn't go through with the wedding.''

Ethan turned back to her, feeling the heat not only of the sun, but of the lingering embarrassment of being left at the altar. ''No, and she couldn't go through with the marriage, either, which probably hurt the most. Hell, we'd been together for two years. I thought we had the kind of close relationship where we could tell each other anything. To know that she'd had these serious doubts all along about settling in a small town and hadn't said anything...'' He shook his head. ''I felt like such a failure after I got over the initial shock and anger.''

''Oh, Ethan, I can't believe you were a failure in your relationship. She was the one who didn't have the courage to be honest with you.''

''Wait. You haven't heard the best part,'' he added with sarcasm. He walked the length of the small area between rocks and bushes, gathering his nerve to finish the tale.

''I went ahead with the move. There was nothing keeping me in Dallas any longer. Ranger Springs was happy to hire me because they wanted to update their police force, bring in new technology and skills. Aunt Bess had been widowed the year before, and she was lonely living by herself in San

Antonio, so I asked if she'd like to move in with me.''

"I'm sure she was a lot of comfort."

Ethan nodded. "She was. I'm close to my parents, but somehow spending time with her made the pain go away faster. She was always there, always seemed to know the right thing to say or do to cheer me up or make me settle down."

"She sounds so much like my Great-aunt Sylvia. I can see why the two are friends."

"Bess liked the town. I began to meet people socially, and one lady in particular. Belinda lived in an even smaller town about seven miles from here, but she came to Ranger Springs to attend a church bazaar one day about a year after Monica and I...broke up." He chuckled at the memory. "I met her when she ran a Stop sign. She was so embarrassed. She had the cleanest driving record I'd ever seen, so I gave her a warning." He looked up at the tips of the cottonwoods, glinting almost silver in the sunlight. "And then I asked her out."

"Oh."

"I don't usually pick up women through my job," he clarified, just in case Robin thought he'd made a habit of hitting on women he stopped...or ones who called about wild animals in the middle of the night. "She was just so darn sweet. She taught preschool at a day-care center in San Marcus. She loved children, loved rural life. She was pretty, too, in a really wholesome sort of way."

He kicked a stone out of his way as he felt his

jaw tense. "So…I asked her to marry me a few months later."

He looked up at Robin to see the expression on her face. He'd expected surprise, even shock, but she looked confused.

"Did you love her?"

"I loved what she stood for. Like you said earlier, I loved the idea of being married, of having a family." Although he'd never lied to Belinda by professing a great, passionate love for her, he'd never been completely honest. Maybe at the time he hadn't realized how caught up he'd been in the fantasy of the perfect small town, the perfect wife. He hadn't been fair to her, and they'd both paid a price.

"Did she accept?"

"Yes, she did. I suppose I was considered a good catch. She was almost thirty, ready to start a family. She was kind of shy, so meeting men didn't come easily to her."

"You aren't married, so obviously something happened."

"History repeated itself," Ethan said bitterly. "We planned a traditional wedding right here in Ranger Springs because the church was larger than in her town. Everything was perfect—or so I thought."

"Don't tell me—"

"Yeah, the same thing happened. I arrived at the church, she didn't. I was frantic with worry— again—and then I got her message." He shook his head at the memories. "At least she was polite enough to send her regrets."

"Oh, Ethan."

"Seems she realized at the last minute that we didn't love each other. She claimed I was so solid and dependable that she thought we'd be a good match, even though we weren't wild about each other...you know. Anyway, she couldn't go through with the wedding. She was sorry that she just couldn't tell me in person."

Robin stuck her chin up a notch. "She didn't have enough backbone for a man like you."

He had to chuckle at her assessment. "We're talking about a two-time loser in the marriage department. Trust me, I wasn't feeling on top of the world at that moment."

"Of course not, but in the long run, it was for the best."

"With about two hundred expectant faces staring at me, though, I didn't appreciate the fact at the time. But to be fair, I should have paid more attention to Belinda. I'm sure that if I'd really loved her, I would have picked up on her reservations about the wedding. I knew she was shy; I should have known she'd have a hard time expressing her opinion. But I really wanted the dream, you know? The happily-ever-after we expect when we decide we're ready to settle down." After what Robin had told him of her reasons for wanting to marry, he believed she, more than anyone else, would understand his feelings.

She held out her hands in an instinctive gesture of comfort. ''You poor guy. Having everyone in town witness the scene at the church must have been so embarrassing for you.''

He settled on the rock next to her. ''One of the reasons I could stay was the support I received from the people here. They were great. Oh, I know they're busybodies most of the time, but they have big hearts. They took me in, made me feel better after I was forced to face some facts about myself.'' He shooed a honeybee away from Robin's hair, his fingers yearning to stroke the soft, golden strands. ''Kind of like you're doing right now.''

She smiled tentatively. ''I can understand because I put someone in the same situation you were in. Or almost the same. I didn't leave Gig standing at the altar, but I did cancel just three weeks before the wedding.''

''Like I said before, you did the right thing. Someday you'll find a man who wants the same life you do, and then you won't run away.''

''I want to believe I'll find that special person, but right now, I'm concentrating more on finding myself. I don't want to go through life doing all the right things and discovering I'm miserable when I'm seventy. Or having regrets for what I should have done.''

Ethan smoothed a strand of Robin's sun-warmed hair back behind her ear. ''A wise person once said that life is not a rehearsal. I believe that. I want to believe I'll have everything I desire from life, but

I'm not in a hurry to make the same mistake again.''

"So make different mistakes," Robin answered softly. "Just don't shut yourself off from life, from happiness.''

She didn't know how alluring she was, with an aura of innocence and freshness that spoke more of her character than a canceled wedding or a broken-hearted fiancé.

He hadn't meant the day to turn out this way. He'd had no intention of touching her, of wanting her. But his hand lingered on her shiny, smooth hair. His gaze was drawn to her perfectly shaped lips. And then he was drowning in her eyes, so warm and welcoming.

He leaned forward, eliminated the distance separating them. He *was* going to make different mistakes, starting right now. Robin closed her eyes and parted her lips, and he was lost, lost, in a kiss that had been nearly two weeks—or maybe a lifetime—in the making.

ROBIN LEANED into the kiss, her thoughts swirling like eddies in the stream, and her emotions soaring like the wispy white clouds overhead. Here, on this heated rock in a deserted Eden, she didn't want to think about yesterdays or tomorrows. She only wanted Ethan's kiss to go on forever. His lips were firm but gentle, his tongue insistent as he pressed closer. She met each thrust with equal fervor, her hunger for this intimacy surprising in its intensity.

His strength shouldn't have surprised her; she'd admired his body on many occasions. But the easy way he lifted her, pulled her across his lap and settled her more tightly against him made her gasp in awe. He covered her lips and continued to kiss her until her head spun and her breath came in shallow puffs.

His hands molded her to him along her back, her shoulders, her hips. She pressed into him, her breasts sensitive and tight against his chest. She wanted him more than she'd ever wanted anything in her life, including the grand wedding, her enjoyable career, her need for family, even her fiancé. Kissing Ethan was real and exciting and...frightening.

She pulled away, panting and wide-eyed. What was she doing? Ethan was a client. She'd tried her best to make that distinction stick this past week. And here she was throwing herself at him, kissing him back, wanting more.

What was happening between them?

"Robin?"

"I...I don't know what just happened."

"Then I must be out of practice. I thought we were kissing."

"That was more than a kiss."

He smiled. "Yeah, I think so, too."

"How did we get from talking to kissing? I thought we weren't going to do anything like that."

"I thought so, too." He didn't seem the least bit

remorseful. In fact, he still held her close. Still looked at her with those intense, sexy eyes.

"You're my client. I don't go around kissing my clients."

"You were my 9-1-1 call. I don't go around kissing women in distress, either."

"I'm not in distress any longer." She shifted on his lap, extremely conscious of the fact he hadn't loosened his grip on her—and that he was more aroused at this moment than he'd been that first night on her front porch. "Does that mean you're not my client any longer?"

"No, I hope you're still working on my house. I don't see that a little kissing has anything to do with our professional relationship."

"You don't?"

"No, I don't. Whatever happened here today isn't going to change your ideas for my living room, is it?"

"Of course not." She shifted again, trying to put a small amount of space between them. But she was in an awkward position, off balance in more ways than one. Ethan's body felt warm, firm, and oh, so good against her chest, stomach and thigh. Her legs dangled over his outspread knee. His hooded blue eyes and kissable lips hovered far too close for her peace of mind.

"Er, do you think you could let me up now? My legs are falling asleep."

"Sorry." He effortlessly shifted her to one knee,

his hands firm around her waist, his fingers straying just a bit lower.

She put both feet on the ground, but felt a little shaky at the moment. She didn't know if she suffered from a lack of blood flow to her legs…or to her brain, which obviously wasn't thinking too clearly.

"I never did tell you why I walked out last night."

His voice penetrated the fog between her ears. Robin forced her thoughts back to the conversation they'd had before the kissing began. "No, I suppose you didn't."

Chapter Ten

Ethan placed his hands under her arms and rose to his feet, supporting her easily. His smile was just as easy, and Robin wanted to believe he felt some tenderness toward her. Some emotion besides friendship. But then she worried that he might feel something more for her, and she wasn't sure she wanted that, either. Darn, but she was confused.

And they still hadn't finished their conversation.

"Okay. I'm listening." She stretched, then walked around the rocks to stare at the stream once again. The scene was peaceful, soothing. She needed calm at the moment; her mind was in turmoil.

"Last night was entirely my fault, Robin," Ethan said from close behind her. "Whatever happened wasn't because you'd been smothering me with design decisions. True, I had no idea you'd need my opinion so much. Since I'd never worked with a decorator before, I assumed you'd pick out things you thought I'd like and just buy them."

"That's not the best method."

"I realize that now. But that night at your place, when I suggested you decorate my house, I didn't know much about how the process worked."

She crossed her arms over her chest, still looking at the scenery instead of him. "So if the decorating wasn't the problem, what was?"

"How I was feeling about you."

She turned around to face Ethan now that she'd slowed her thumping heart and stilled the tingling in her lips. "What do you mean?"

"When you first came to town and mentioned the wedding that almost happened, I immediately thought of the two women who'd stood me up at the altar. Oh, you didn't look like them—they were as different from you as night and day. But the situation seemed similar. I didn't expect to like you."

"Then why did you ask me to dinner?"

He rubbed the back of his neck. "I have to admit that was your great-aunt's doing. She called to talk to Bess, who'd gone to San Antonio. Sylvia was worried about you, Robin. She asked that I look after you as a favor."

"That stinker! She had no business involving you."

Ethan shook his head. "I didn't see it that way. Bess and Sylvia are good friends. I couldn't turn my back on a very reasonable request. Besides, I had a really good time."

"I enjoyed myself, too, but that's not the point. You wouldn't have gotten involved if my great-aunt

Sylvia hadn't asked you.'' Robin threw up her hands in exasperation. "You'd think I was ten years old.''

Ethan smiled. "No one would think that.''

"Well, I'm not real happy with my great-aunt at the moment.''

"How do you feel about me?''

"I'm not angry at you. You were just being a nice guy. As a matter of fact, I told myself that very same thing. I recognized that you were very polite.''

"Don't make me out to be some kind of martyr. I didn't suffer through our dates.''

"They weren't dates.''

He shrugged. "Whatever you call sharing time together, having a meal. The point is, I didn't mind asking you to dinner.''

"I realize that, but you wouldn't have called me without someone else's interference.''

"Robin, I haven't dated anyone in a long time. That's one reason my aunt is always encouraging me to go out, have some fun. You probably don't realize this because you haven't been in town very long, but I actually live a very boring life.''

Ethan, boring? He was exaggerating, of course. "She did mention something about you sitting at home too much.''

"She what?''

Robin grimaced. Now she'd done it; given away Bess's confidence. "Your aunt and I kind of talked before she left. She mentioned that you'd probably sit at home and watch television, or just go in to the office and work too much, while she was gone.''

He narrowed his eyes. ''Is that why you asked me over to dinner?''

Robin felt like squirming. ''That might have had something to do with it. But,'' she quickly added, ''I also had a good time when we went to dinner and wanted to thank you.''

''I have a feeling our aunts have been talking to each other as well as to us individually.''

''You think they hatched some kind of conspiracy to get us together?''

''Sounds like it to me.''

''I can't believe either one of them would think I was ready for dating. Good grief, I'd just dumped my fiancé three weeks before our wedding!''

''It does seem a little far-fetched they thought someone with my history would be an ideal candidate for a date with you.''

That stung a bit, although she understood his position. Someone who'd been dumped twice—not weeks before, but at the actual altar—certainly wouldn't jump at the chance to get involved with a woman who'd done almost the same thing to her fiancé.

Ethan rubbed his jaw. ''We've gotten off the subject again.''

''You're right. Please, finish telling me why you walked out last night.''

''Robin, I walked out that night not because I

was irritated with you, but because I discovered I genuinely liked you. From what happened today, I'm sure you can guess, I also found you attractive. Of course, I thought about the similarities in our pasts—''

His shoulder-mounted radio unit blared loudly in the peace of the idyllic summer glade.

''Dispatch to Parker. Chief, we have a situation at the Kash 'n' Karry.''

He depressed the button. ''I'm on my way.'' Ethan turned to Robin. ''We have to go now. We'll talk more later, okay?''

''Sure,'' she said, as he grasped her hand and led her toward the police car. Except now she was more confused than ever, and she had a sneaking suspicion that she wasn't going to like what he had to say.

As they roared down the gravel road toward the highway, the only conclusion she could reach from their conversation was that Ethan was going to tell her he desired her, he liked her, but...

ETHAN WASN'T REAL HAPPY to take Robin along to the Kash 'n' Karry, but he didn't have an option. She was quiet as he drove as fast as possible down the farm-to-market road toward the intersection with the state highway. Probably scared to death, he thought. He tried to explain that he wasn't endangering her life by taking her into an active crime scene, but his sketchy description as they sped down the two-lane road seemed to fall on deaf ears.

Nothing could be farther from the truth. He and his dispatchers had worked out a code for "situations" involving Crazy Ed Kaminsky. But explaining the older man to someone unfamiliar with his escapades wasn't easy.

"Here we are," he said, as they pulled into the lot. "Why don't you stay in the car. This shouldn't take long."

She craned her neck, rising up from the seat to see through the multiple posters, signs and advertisements that littered the glass entry into the convenience store. "Whatever you say."

He smiled as he strolled through the door that never did close all the way. As he expected, Crazy Ed stood near the checkout counter, this time clutching a package of cupcakes and a bag of dry dog food.

"What's going on, Mr. Kaminsky?"

"I told him to put this on my account, and the darn fool doesn't understand!" His rheumy blue eyes appeared wild, but Ethan knew Crazy Ed was harmless. Unfortunately, it was sometimes difficult to convince a new clerk at the convenience store of that fact.

"This looks like a new person," Ethan said as he nodded toward the teenage clerk. "I'll bet they don't understand your account."

"What's wrong with businesses anymore? Don't they want their regular customers?"

"It's just a mistake, Mr. Kaminsky. Why don't

you wait for me by the door, and I'll straighten all this out.''

''About time somebody did,'' the old man grumbled as he shuffled off in his bedroom slippers and 1970s-era, high-water jogging pants.

Once Crazy Ed was out of earshot, Ethan pulled out his wallet. ''How much does he owe?''

''Four twenty-nine,'' the wide-eyed teenager said. ''Does he really do this often?''

''Only when he gets out from under the nose of his daughter. Don't worry—he's harmless. He needs to be in a nursing home, but she can't afford one. And Mr. Kaminsky won't give up his dog, so that's another problem.''

''Do you always pay out of your own pocket?''

''His daughter will pay me back.'' Ethan slid his wallet back in place. ''Thanks for not panicking. You did the right thing by calling. I don't like him out walking around, so I'd rather take care of it and give him a ride home.''

''Okay. Thanks.''

Ethan walked to the door. ''How about a ride home, Mr. Kaminsky? I'll bet you haven't had lunch yet.''

''Yeah, my daughter'll be lookin' for me,'' he grumbled.

Robin appeared surprised when the two of them approached the car, but she didn't say a thing about the unusual circumstances. When Ethan whispered in her ear that they were giving Crazy Ed a ride home, she just nodded and politely answered the older man's questions, which ranged from whether she had a dog to whether she was a criminal under arrest.

After dropping off Crazy Ed and talking to his daughter, Ethan explained a bit of the "situation" the old man caused occasionally, then took Robin back to the municipal building. Again, she appeared quiet, but he didn't have time to talk right now, anyway. He had a staff meeting at three o'clock that he had to get ready for.

"I'll give you a call, okay?" he said, as Robin settled into her sporty coupe.

"Sure," she replied, putting on one of her big, fake smiles. He didn't know why, but her struggle to remain polite and cheerful hurt him more than he wanted to acknowledge.

ROBIN POURED HERSELF a glass of wine and settled onto the sofa. She should be working on sketches for Ethan's home, but she didn't feel like immersing herself in a project she wasn't sure she'd see through to completion. Instead of thinking about Ethan or his house, she clicked on the television and tried to get involved in the rerun of a sitcom she'd never watched to begin with.

She was frowning and sipping her wine when the doorbell rang—and she almost sloshed the golden liquid on Mrs. Franklin's couch. She hadn't heard anyone pull up, but then, who could, over the canned laughter on the television sitcom?

As she passed by the window, she pulled back a

sheer to see Ethan's black Bronco sitting in the driveway. Her heart immediately started racing and her hopes leaped...until she remembered he was probably here to finish the conversation about how he didn't want to be around her any longer.

She swung the door open. "Hello. Come in."

He pulled open the storm door and stepped inside. He looked as good now as he had earlier; all crisply starched uniform and neatly trimmed hair. She couldn't read his expression—not an unusual situation, since he kept tight control over himself.

"How are you?"

Bored silly. "Fine. Did you have any more problems with Mr. Kaminsky?"

"No. The rest of my day was fairly uneventful."

Ethan looked uncomfortable, she thought. "You handled him really well. Some people would have locked him up, I'm sure."

"He's not dangerous—at least not yet. I hope his medication continues to help his condition. I've heard stories about him when he was younger. He was in World War II in the Pacific, and he's been active in the VFW for years. I think it's sad, maybe tragic, that he's reduced to shuffling around in house slippers."

"You respect him."

Ethan shrugged. "I respect what he stood for. People who are willing to give their lives for their country have my admiration."

"Well, whatever his situation, I wanted you to

know I admired your treatment of Mr. Kaminsky. You have a kind heart.''

"Don't make me into some kind of angel. I'm not.''

"I'm simply trying to give you a compliment.''

He smiled just a bit. "Sorry. I'm a little uncomfortable, I suppose, but thanks.'' His smile faded. "We didn't get to finish our conversation.''

"No, I suppose we didn't.''

"Would you like to have dinner?''

She felt as though she'd been punched. As soon as she thought she had Ethan figured out, he did something to startle her. Like his kiss earlier today. The one that had blown her socks off. And now this invitation.

"Did you get another call from one of our aunts?'' she quipped, trying to keep the conversation light.

Ethan shifted his weight to one leg and grimaced. "*Ouch.* No, I didn't. I'd like to have the opportunity to finish the conversation we started earlier, and I'd like to share a meal with you.''

"This isn't a pity date?''

"No, it isn't. Why in the world would you think I pitied you?''

"That's not what I meant. I suppose it was just a figure of speech.''

"So, do you want to have dinner?''

"Okay.'' She looked down at her jeans and striped cotton shirt. "Do I need to change?''

"No, you're fine.''

"Then let me grab my purse." She walked into the kitchen and found her small zippered bag, slipped on the sandals she'd abandoned earlier and walked back into the living room.

Ethan was standing by the window, his back to her. He had a great backside.

"I'm ready."

He turned around, his expression thoughtful. But then he smiled as though everything in his world was routine, even cheerful.

"Let's go," he said.

ETHAN HAD BEEN to Bretford House a dozen times with his aunt, members of the city council, and once for a Chamber of Commerce dinner. The restaurant was in an old frame house with a rock foundation and chimney. The grounds had been landscaped, including a small gazebo where an occasional wedding was performed. Tonight the gravel parking lot, which had been the side yard when the house was a residence, had enough empty spaces that he knew they'd have a table inside.

"I haven't been here before," Robin said, as he opened her door.

"The restaurant is fairly new by Ranger Springs standards—maybe two years old. The owner is a former chef from Fort Worth. He's used the living room, dining room and bedrooms for separate dining areas, and everything looks kind of old-fashioned." The word *romantic* came to mind, but he pushed it aside for now. He didn't know how

Robin would react to such a statement, so he added, "I think you'll like the food."

Within a minute they were inside and seated. On the way to the table, he'd nodded or said hello to a half-dozen people he recognized. Ralph Biggerstaff was there with his wife of many years. Thelma was having dinner with her daughter, who'd divorced her cheating husband and moved back to town earlier this year.

He was getting to be as big a busybody as the rest of the town, except that he kept his observations and categorizations to himself. The way everyone was surreptitiously looking at Robin and him, he knew the rumor mill would be buzzing tomorrow.

"What's good?" Robin asked as she opened the two-page menu.

"I've had the steak. Aunt Bess said the smoked chicken is great."

She nodded and went back to studying the choices, as though she were terribly interested in food at the moment. Maybe she was. Maybe she was avoiding him and their conversation as long as possible.

When their waitress came to the table, they ordered wine with their meals. Ethan settled back into his chair, steepling his fingers as he studied Robin across the tiny vase of flowers and the votive candle. "This has been a long day for you, hasn't it."

She appeared thoughtful. "An eventful day. I've had busier."

"In Houston."

She nodded. "Preparing show homes, attending market with clients, then trying to look fresh at parties later. Sometimes the decorating profession can be very trying."

"There's nothing like show homes or decorating markets in Ranger Springs."

"No," she said thoughtfully. "Life here is certainly different."

He wanted to ask whether life was better or worse here, but the waitress brought their wine, then left with the promise their salads would be out shortly. Having second thoughts, he decided perhaps he didn't want to know the answer. He didn't want to pry unnecessarily into her personal life or opinions, he told himself.

Robin sipped her wine. "I don't suppose my professional or personal activities compare to the life-and-death choices you might have to make."

He was grateful for the change in subject. "*Might* is the key word. The potential for danger is always there—we train for it constantly. Fortunately, no one on the force in Ranger Springs has had to face a serious felony with weapons drawn."

"Really? That's saying a lot about the community."

"It's a good town. That's why I chose their offer when I decided to leave the Bureau."

Their salads came then, forestalling more serious conversation. As Ethan speared his lettuce and tomato, he knew that he'd have to finally say the words that would put his relationship with Robin on the back burner. He had to ignore the searing kiss they'd shared this afternoon…and focus again on the reasons why they had no future.

Throughout the meal, they commented on their entrées, the decor and the various people who seemed to be staring at them. Robin declined dessert, but he stalled a few minutes more because he was having a pretty good time, despite the reason for the date. Over coffee and a piece of pecan pie for him, Ethan mentally rehearsed what he'd say.

But not here in the restaurant. What had seemed like a good idea earlier, was, in reality, foolish. How could he concentrate on Robin with half the town looking over his shoulder or straining to hear his words?

"Why don't we take a walk through the garden."

AFTER THE SUN SET, the temperature dropped slowly to a bearable range. Walking out of the air-conditioned restaurant into the Texas night, Robin felt the residual heat of the day, but she was much more comfortable than she had been with the sun beating down on her. Like at the stream at midday… On that heated rock beside Ethan…

She had to quit thinking about that kiss.

"Would you like to sit?" he asked, as they reached the gazebo.

"Sure." Bad news was always received better sitting down.

Ethan sat across from her, leaning forward with

his forearms on his knees, his hands clasped. He appeared a bit nervous, but resolute.

He'd come to the conclusion the kiss was a bad idea. No doubt about it.

"Robin, you know by now that I think you're a very attractive woman."

She nodded.

"I probably left you with the wrong impression earlier about my intentions."

Here it comes. The explanation. The withdrawal.

"Ethan, you don't have to explain yourself. I understand."

"I know you understand about my former fiancées and my desire to live in a small town, but I'm not sure I made myself clear about how you fit into the picture."

Robin tilted her head and looked intently at him. "I *don't* fit into the picture."

"That's a blunt way to say it, but, yes, I suppose that's right." He leaned back on the gazebo's wooden seat. "Ranger Springs could hardly support a decorator, and besides, I can't see you giving up your life in Houston to settle in a place like this."

She felt herself grow heated over his presumption. "I see. You've made a lot of assumptions about me, haven't you?"

"I didn't mean to sound critical. I'm not. Small-town life isn't for everyone."

Obviously he'd decided it wasn't for *her*. "I realize that."

"And I'm not going to leave here. So as much as I enjoy being around you, I can't see a long-term relationship."

Chapter Eleven

"Apparently you can't see *any* type of relationship."

He stiffened. "I'm the chief of police here, in a position of authority and in the spotlight from several angles. I can't afford to have a hot, temporary affair."

She felt the heat increase on her cheeks and neck, and knew she was blushing. Thank goodness for the darkness. "I don't remember consenting to a hot affair."

He ran a hand through his hair. "I didn't mean to imply you had. I'm just trying to be honest."

"What, exactly, are you saying?"

He leaned forward again, this time reaching for and capturing her hands. "I'd like nothing better than to indulge in a wonderful, mutually satisfying, hot and heavy relationship with you. For two weeks. For two months. But I can't. I just want you to understand."

"I think I've understood this from the beginning. You're the one who seems confused."

He straightened, letting go of her hands. "What do you mean?"

"You're the one who almost kissed me in the car, ran out of your house, and kissed me beside the stream. Ethan, I haven't been throwing myself at you."

He pushed off the bench and began to pace. "I know you haven't." He stopped, then turned to face her. The faint light from the windows of the restaurant illuminated his features. "You didn't have to do a thing. I wanted you the first time I saw you in the doorway of the Franklin house."

She leaned against the post of the gazebo and folded her arms beneath her breasts. She remembered his comforting embrace. His hardness. His arousal. Now her heat increased. "Well, thanks, I suppose. I didn't know I'd ever inspired that kind of passion."

He shook his head. "I can't speak for the rest of the male population. Maybe they're blind. I felt a strong attraction to you from the beginning."

"I felt the same for you, too, although I was confused. I didn't want a relationship any more than you did. I thought we'd made that clear to each other."

"It seemed to me the rules changed this afternoon."

"If they did, *you* changed them."

"Which is why I wanted to tell you again that I didn't want to send the wrong signals."

She frowned in skepticism. "You said earlier it was only a kiss."

He ran a hand through his hair again. "I lied. You tied me in knots. I felt like I'd been caught up in a Texas twister."

She felt some feminine smugness at his admission. "But you don't want to do anything about it."

"Wrong. I *want* to. Believe me, I really want to. But I can't. It wouldn't be fair to you, me or the people who care about us."

"I'm not in the habit of asking for anyone else's opinion when I make a decision."

"And I'm in the habit of looking at how my decisions will be perceived by the citizens of this town." He visibly stiffened. "If that sounds boring or unsophisticated to you, I'm sorry."

She wanted to jump up and run out of the gazebo, but she didn't. How far could you run from the chief of police in a town this small? "Then you're right—you shouldn't have a summer affair with a flighty decorator from Houston." She held up a hand. "Even if she were offering."

Ethan smiled tentatively. "I didn't mean to sound like I was taking you for granted."

"You made me sound like a sure thing."

"I'm sorry. I was going at this from my point of view."

Typically male, she wanted to say, but she didn't. "I'm glad we have that out in the open. My only question is this—do you want me to continue with the house, as you said this afternoon, or have you had second thoughts about that, too?''

''No, I really like your ideas. I'd love for you to continue with the decorating.'' He jammed his hands into his pockets. ''Is there any way you can proceed without me being involved so much?''

Robin took in a deep breath, hiding the hurt of his withdrawal as best she could. ''Of course. Give me a budget, and I'll only need to consult with you on major purchases.''

''I can do that.''

''I will need your input occasionally.''

''Just let me know when and where, and I'll be glad to cooperate.''

''We'll need to go some places together. Not of-ten—but if I see a large piece that I believe will be perfect, I'll want your approval.''

''Sure.'' He walked toward her, then took a seat beside her this time. ''Look, I didn't mean to sound like I couldn't be around you. I just think it would be best if we limited our private time together.''

''To avoid temptation,'' she finished for him.

He looked at her in the dim light, his features softening. ''Yes.''

His voice sounded so sexy and rough that she almost leaned toward him and captured his lips once more. Just to see if he was right. Just to see if this afternoon had been a fluke. The realization of how much she wanted him hit her hard, and she jumped up from the bench.

"We'd better be getting home," she said quickly. "I'm sure you have an early morning."

He straightened as if he, too, had suddenly become aware of the intimate setting. "Of course."

They walked in silence to the Bronco, and drove to the Franklin house with only polite chitchat and observations between them.

In the driveway, as Ethan cut the engine, Robin reached for the door handle. "Thank you for dinner, Ethan."

"I'll walk you to the door."

"You don't have to—" she started to say, but he was already out of the vehicle and walking around to her side.

They walked side by side to the front door. Robin felt the awkwardness of the situation like never before. Before, she'd experienced the underlying attraction and anticipation. Tonight, she felt the suppression of emotion between them.

This feeling was much worse.

"Thank you for having dinner with me," Ethan said, as Robin fit the key in the lock.

"You're welcome." She pushed open the heavy wood door. "I imagine your aunt will be back soon."

"Yes, I'm expecting her any day."

"That's good. I know she worries about your being alone."

Ethan shrugged. "I'm a grown man, but sometimes she sees me as someone much younger."

"I know what you mean. My great-aunt is the

same. If our aunts were different, they wouldn't have pushed us toward each other in their not-so-subtle way.''

He nodded, then took a deep breath. ''Aunt Bess doesn't understand why I'm reluctant to get involved again, but I do have a position in the community. I can't go from woman to woman, getting involved and uninvolved on a whim.''

Robin shook her head. ''She's wrong.'' So very, very wrong. ''I can't imagine a woman around who wouldn't jump at the chance to spend time with you.''

''Right,'' he scoffed. ''They just don't want to marry me.''

''Oh, Ethan, that's not true.''

''Isn't it? Look at my history.''

''Whatever happened between you and those two other women wasn't because you're unexciting. Believe me, I'm a really good judge of people. You are *not* boring.''

''I'm glad I have one person on my side,'' he said with a touch of dark humor.

She shook her head again, but could tell he wasn't convinced. And what could she do to show him how exciting he was to her? Certainly nothing that fell within the bounds of the much cooler relationship he'd defined earlier.

''Well, if I can't convince you, I suppose I'll just say good-night,'' she said, when he remained stoic and silent.

There was a brief pause, then he leaned forward

and gave her a sisterly peck on the cheek. He pulled away quickly, smiled awkwardly, and turned to walk toward his Bronco.

She placed her palm where his lips had touched her cheek. "Good night, Ethan," Robin whispered into the silence of the night, but she felt as though she was saying goodbye to something very special.

BESS HADN'T BEEN HOME twenty-four hours when she decided to have lunch at the Four Square Café to get caught up on all the news. Specifically, news about Ethan and Robin, since her nephew wasn't talking...darn it!

She walked in and looked around, immediately spotting Thelma and Joyce sitting at their usual table, as thick as thieves. Those two could gossip like no one else. She hurried toward them, intent on joining the conversation.

Thelma's eyes lit up. "Bess! When did you get back?"

"Yesterday afternoon. It's good to be home."

"Did you have a good time?" Joyce asked.

"A wonderful time. It's good to visit with old friends." Bess sighed as she reached for a menu. "Of course, I always miss Ethan, and I worry about him being by himself for that long." She glanced up briefly from perusing the menu she already knew by heart.

Thelma and Joyce exchanged meaningful glances, then Joyce said, "He hasn't been alone all that much."

Bess tried to appear shocked. "What do you mean?"

The waitress came then and took their orders. Bess tried to hide her impatience to get back to the subject.

"Ethan didn't tell you?"

"Tell me what?"

The ladies proceeded to tell her about Ethan's dates with Robin—from Wimberley to the latest at Bretford House. They seemed to take a lot of pleasure in the gossip, but then they became more serious.

"We're glad Ethan is seeing someone again, Bess. But a decorator from Houston? She's only here temporarily."

"Who says? She might decide to stay."

"She seems a little ill-equipped to live here. Why, I don't think she can even cook! She tried to buy one of those fancy catered meals here in Ranger Springs." Joyce leaned closer. "Probably for your nephew."

Bess winced inwardly. That was her fault. She should have listened to Sylvia, who'd told her Robin couldn't cook.

Thelma added, "We'd all like to see Ethan find someone suitable, but I'm not sure this young lady is the one."

"I've known her great aunt for a long time," said Bess. "Robin is really a very level-headed young woman."

"If you say so," Joyce said, patting Bess's hand.

"But remember, she is a decorator. You know how...unreliable those artistic types can be."

ETHAN ARRIVED HOME to the welcome scent of fresh-baked rolls and pot roast. He knew he'd missed his aunt, but smelling her cooking made the sentiment that much sharper. He placed his hat on the peg beside the back door and walked through the kitchen.

"Aunt Bess, I'm home."

"In here."

He found her in the living room, arms folded beneath her breasts, staring at the fireplace wall. "What's the matter?"

"Robin dropped off some sketches this afternoon. I'm trying to imagine what the brick would look like painted."

"Robin came by the house?"

"Yes, she did. She said she didn't want to bother you when you were home, so she chose the afternoon."

"Really?" Ethan tried to appear casual, but as usual, the thought of Robin standing here earlier caused his pulse rate to increase a notch. "How was she?"

"She's fine. Oh, a little quieter than I remembered, maybe."

"Quieter? She's not sick, is she?"

"No." Bess chuckled. "My memory is probably failing me. She just seemed a little more...animated last time I saw her."

Ethan felt the guilt kick in. He'd caused her sparkle to dim, but he didn't know what to do about it. The best approach was to avoid the subject, he supposed, so he went back to the reason for Robin's visit.

"She doesn't like the brick?"

"No, she said it was too dated. Tan brick isn't 'in' any longer. She thinks we should paint it to match the wall. She suggested a warm, kind of golden-beige color for the living room and a terracotta for the dining room."

Ethan stood beside his aunt. "Gee, I don't know. I guess she's right." He leaned over and kissed Bess's forehead. "It's good to have you back."

"I'm glad to be back," she said, patting his hand. "Although I'm not sure my temperament is going to tolerate much of this decorating."

"If you don't want me to change things, I'll call her and cancel."

"No!" Bess sounded alarmed. "I didn't mean that at all. I think what she has planned will be great."

"But you don't like the fireplace idea?"

"Come to think of it, I like it fine." She turned to him and smiled. "Why don't you get changed, and I'll get the meal on the table."

"Fine by me," he said, already heading for the hall. "I'll clean up."

Aunt Bess was a sweetheart, he decided as he headed for the master bedroom. Even if she didn't like what Robin had planned, she'd never stop him from making the changes. Bess wanted him to be happy, and if decorating the house in a style Robin called "Southwestern country" was the answer, then Bess would go along.

He suspected she'd rather have the fussy type of furniture she'd used in her room, but she'd never suggest it for him. Thank goodness.

Robin, on the other hand, wanted him to be very satisfied with his choices.

What had started out as a way for her to stay busy and out of his hair had backfired, and the only person he could blame was himself. However, he felt their talk the other night, despite the parts where he'd blown it, had gone well. She understood why he couldn't get involved, why he didn't want a casual summer fling.

Oh, hell, he admitted to himself as he stripped off the uniform shirt, of course he wanted a summer affair. But he was afraid he wouldn't want it to end come August or September. He'd want Robin in his life—and what kind of pain would that cause? Lots.

He hadn't been madly in love with Belinda, his second fiancée, and look at the damage her rejection had caused. The town had rallied around him, but for at least six months after the botched wedding, their sympathetic looks and well-meaning but probing questions left him gritting his teeth in frustrated anger. And Belinda? She'd never come back to Ranger Springs to shop or visit, as far as he knew. Now, two years later, he felt foolish for thinking their marriage might work, and sympathy toward a shy young woman who didn't deserve to be shunned by the town she enjoyed visiting.

He probably hadn't really been in love with Monica, either, although it had seemed like the real thing at the time. After all, if he'd really loved her, he would have found a way to compromise around her career. He did feel some lingering anger over the way she'd dumped him, though. Monica was an intelligent, take-charge kind of woman. She should have had the guts to tell him to his face that she didn't want to marry him and live in Ranger Springs. If *she'd* loved *him,* she would have, wouldn't she?

He pulled off his boots, then his pants. No, he probably hadn't really been in love yet. But with Robin, he sensed the potential for profound emotion. For extreme want. For overwhelming need. If he gave in to his desires, he might fall hard and fast, and what good would that do? He'd be left brokenhearted and alone at the end of the summer. He balled up his uniform and tossed it into the laundry hamper with unnecessary force.

Controlling the situation now was the best approach, he told himself as he pulled on jeans and a T-shirt. He and Robin would be polite, but not close friends. And when she left, she wouldn't take his heart.

ROBIN STEERED HER CART down the produce aisle, her thoughts on colors and textures of the fruit and vegetables—anything that kept her from thinking about how lonely the past few days had been. She missed Ethan with an intensity that was both anticipated and surprising. Oh, she'd known she'd feel sadness that they couldn't, or wouldn't, explore the attraction between them. But she hadn't expected the sense of loss she felt almost every waking moment.

She was working on his house, but not with him any longer. She was around his things, but not around him. She smelled his scent throughout his rooms, on his belongings, and she wanted to hear his voice and see his face again.

But she wasn't going to give in to her desires and use any excuse to spend time with him. Why torture herself? He'd made his feelings clear. As an adult, she needed to respect his right to avoid commitments. To avoid her.

She was so distracted by her thoughts that she ran her cart into a display of lemons and limes, sending fruit rolling across the linoleum floor like bright bowling balls in search of a target.

Moaning, she parked her cart out of the way and bent down to gather the yellow and green fruit. She wasn't in any hurry; she had nowhere to go, no one to see. She just didn't like the fact that her fascination—and yes, frustration—with Ethan had left her incapable of navigating a grocery store.

She heard footsteps, but ignored the other shoppers to find the last two limes. One rolled at the touch of her fingertips, coming to rest against one highly polished boot. She reached for the fruit, but the owner of the boot neatly and gently placed it over the lime.

She realized she was staring at well-creased cotton pants above the black boots. Who wore black and blue together? *The police.* She moaned, knowing—just *knowing*—who would be looking down in amusement at her.

"Ethan," she whispered, closing her eyes. She didn't want to see him now. She wasn't ready.

"Hello, Robin." He removed his boot from the unscathed lime and hunkered down in front of her.

His face was close, his familiar scent invading her mind until she couldn't breath for fear that she'd overload on his presence. A faint shadow of beard covered his jaw, and she imagined there would be just a trace of scratchiness if she placed her palm on his cheek.

"What are you doing here?" she whispered.

"Shopping for a few things Aunt Bess needed," he replied, nodding toward a hand basket Robin hadn't noticed earlier. "And we're in the grocery, not the library," he added with a touch of amusement. "You don't have to whisper."

She felt a blush start on her neck and creep up her face. To hide her reaction, she broke eye contact and retrieved the lime. "I'll just finish up here and let you get back to your shopping."

His hand stilled hers. "How are you?" he asked, his tone now serious and gentle.

"I'm fine," she answered brightly, forcing a smile. "I ran out of a few things and thought I'd go before I forgot. You know how early everything closes around here.''

''Yeah,'' he said, his voice flat. ''Not like the big city.''

''That's right.'' Robin pushed to her feet, her legs prickling from hunching down on the floor. Or maybe she was just as shaky as she'd been the other day beside the stream, after Ethan had kissed her.

She didn't want to believe his mere presence could affect her so. She didn't want him to have that much power, because she was leaving here in a month and a half—maybe sooner—to go back to her comfortable, familiar life. If she became too close to Ethan, she wouldn't have any more peace in Houston than she'd had before she left for Ranger Springs. The main difference would be the man she left behind—the man who affected her more than the fiancé she'd dumped after two years of courtship.

Ethan continued to squat, looking up with piercing blue eyes and a troubled expression. Then he rose and retrieved his basket. ''Let me know if you need anything…for the decorating project or whatever.''

''Of course,'' she said, proud that her voice remained level. Ethan would never know how much he affected her, she silently vowed. Admitting her attraction would only make him uneasy, and besides, she didn't want to humiliate herself.

''Please, tell Bess hello for me,'' she said as she smiled and placed the last lime back in the display.

Without a backward glance, she pushed her shopping cart down the aisle and away from the man who had the good sense and steely disposition not to get involved.

BESS CALLED SYLVIA that afternoon and explained the conversation at the Four Square Café, then what she'd seen with her own eyes.

"I went away, expecting to find them all cozy and involved when I got back. But they're not! She's decorating his living room and dining room, but that's all that's going on."

"Are you sure? These young people can be pretty sneaky."

"Look who's talking! I can't see that you've lost your ability to sneak around."

"This is different, Bess."

"Of course it is," she said rather sarcastically. "We're talking about our great-niece and nephew's happiness."

"Exactly. So what are you going to do?"

"I want to see them together so I can find out what's wrong. I think Ethan's entirely over that last marriage fiasco, but what if he's not? And poor Robin must still be upset. How did her parents and fiancé take it?"

"I think they are in denial of how she truly feels. All they saw was the enormous amount of money that was wasted. Forfeited deposits to florists, the band and the country club. The wedding gown. The invitations." Sylvia sighed. "The wedding was going to be a huge social event for Warren and

Robin's parents. You just can't imagine what a ruckus her cancellation caused.''

"I hadn't really thought about the differences between a small wedding, like the one Ethan's fiancée had planned, and a much larger one in Houston."

"There is a huge difference just in the scale. Add to that the heated feelings involved, and it was a whopper of a mess."

"Is there a possibility she hasn't discussed *why* she couldn't marry what's-his-name?''

"Warren—but everyone calls him Gig."

"And what about Warren? Did Robin talk to him after she broke off the engagement?''

"No, I'm sure she didn't. He was pretty upset. I think he tried to convince her that she was just emotional, like all brides. He didn't want to hear how she felt.''

"Hmm. Maybe Robin really isn't ready to move on, then. Maybe we're pushing her into something she isn't prepared for.''

"You may be right, although I still feel sure your nephew would be good for her.''

"Not if she's not ready."

"What can we do?''

"I think she needs to talk to her parents. If her fiancé will sit down with her and act decently, then she should try again to explain her reasons.''

"Easier said than done," Sylvia said. "I don't think Robin is ready to come back to Houston.''

"Maybe the time's not right.''

"Maybe," Bess hedged, "but Sylvia, I'm not giving up on those two.''

Chapter Twelve

The invitation to lunch couldn't have come at a better time. When Bess called her, Robin had just located a good source for the type of custom, square coffee table she wanted for The Project. The furniture maker was in Fredericksburg, so she couldn't go to see him right now. Since the actual renovation was under way, she wanted to make the best use of her time so she could finish quickly. So she wouldn't be forced to spend hours with Ethan...and want even more.

Grabbing her purse, plans and keys, she hurried to her car. Bess had asked if Robin would drive them to Bretford House, since her car was in the shop.

She hadn't realized until Ethan had clearly expressed his intention not to get involved, how much she missed having at least one friend around. With Bess back in town, the stay in Ranger Springs would go much faster. Perhaps Bess would even like to give her input on the decorating. With Bess's approval, Robin wouldn't have to bother Ethan as much. And if they weren't near each other, he wouldn't "bother" her.

Besides, he should like not having to deal with any personal decisions.

Alone. That's what he wanted, she thought as she slid behind the wheel. The man would probably find one excuse after another to stay single. After all, he'd claimed he was boring to women! Hogwash, as his aunt would say. He didn't want to risk his heart again, which was fine with her. She wasn't about to hope for something that wasn't going to happen.

She knew the way to Ethan's house so well that the trip took mere minutes. There was no car in the driveway, so Ethan was at work. Good. Today, she just wanted to have a friendly visit with Bess, and celebrate finding a good furniture source.

When Bess answered the door, Robin hugged her, then they set out for the restaurant.

The tables in the main dining room were sparsely occupied, but the bigger room to the side was full.

"Is that a club?" Robin asked Bess.

"The Fourth of July Committee," Bess explained. "That's our biggest single event of the year, although the Christmas candlelighting is getting popular, too."

Robin smiled. Apparently Ranger Springs wasn't too concerned about being politically correct. In Houston the appropriate term would be "holiday candlelighting."

They chatted about the decorating. They talked

about Bess's friends in San Antonio, about Sylvia, about Robin's stay in the Franklin house. In fact, they talked about everything *but* Ethan Parker.

And then, as if the scene were staged by a Hollywood studio, he walked through the door. His gaze zeroed in on her as he stepped into the room, and her heart skipped a beat. He was coming straight to their table.

"AUNT BESS, you didn't tell me you were going out to lunch today," Ethan said as he leaned down to kiss his aunt's cheek.

"I didn't know I had to report my every move, dear boy," she chided.

He straightened and watched Robin sip some water. *Hiding her nerves,* he would have said about a suspect. But what was she nervous about? Surely she didn't think he'd have a serious discussion with her in this restaurant…again. Or perhaps that's what was causing her anxiety—the memory of their trip here a few days ago. Or was she still flustered about their encounter at the grocery store?

"How are you?" he said. His words came out far more soft and intimate than he intended. He wanted to look his fill, but he had to settle for a casual glance, since his aunt was staring at him. Robin was wearing a floral sundress with straps so tiny that he wondered what she was wearing beneath it. Surely she had a bra on. No one went out to lunch at Bretford House without a bra.

Damn, he wanted to know, even as he told himself it was none of his business.

"I'm fine. Bess and I were just talking about the decorating project."

"Really?" He turned to his aunt, trying to blank out the image of Robin in a scrap of a clingy dress and nothing else. What were they talking about? Ah, yes: the decorating project. "Robin has some good ideas, don't you think?" he forced himself to say.

"Yes, I like what she has in mind. She's such a clever young woman."

Robin seemed uncomfortable, so he changed the subject. "I'm meeting with the committee," he said, nodding toward the separate room. Just as he had the other night in his house, he needed to get away before he did or said something stupid in front of his aunt and half the town.

"I hope the plans are going well. Do you know if we're having those adorable lion and tiger cubs again this year? I thought that was such a good fund-raising idea."

"I'm not sure, Aunt Bess. I'll ask."

"While you're at it, tell them we don't need a car for every different little miss beauty queen. It drags out the parade too long."

"I'll tell them, although I don't know why you don't get on the committee each year. You always have your share of ideas."

"Oh, I don't have time for that committee. They

meet far too often for my taste. I've got better things to do with my time."

Ethan smiled as he edged backward toward the committee luncheon. "Well, I'd better be going."

Robin smiled in that way he'd recognized as phony, although she probably had no idea anyone could tell she wasn't sincere.

"It was nice seeing you again," she said.

"Same here. Like I said, let me know when you need my approval on something."

"I may get Bess to help on some things."

"Really?" He was surprised at how disappointed he felt. Was it possible he was looking forward to seeing what selections she made for him? Or did he subconsciously want to spend more time with her, even though he knew logically he shouldn't.

Frustrated and confused, he still had to be civil…and bland. Especially for Aunt Bess. She couldn't guess how much he'd grown to like Robin in the past two weeks. His efforts were minimal at best; he was sure his smile was as artificial as Robin's. "That's great."

ETHAN ARRIVED HOME to find his aunt folding her laundry. "Getting settled back in from your trip?" he asked as he hung his hat on the peg beside the back door.

"Actually, I'm getting ready to go on another one."

"You're kidding. You just got home day before yesterday."

"I know, but I called Sylvia last night, and she's rather lonely since Robin isn't around. She wondered if I could come and visit, and I thought that might be a good idea, with all this decorating going on."

"I didn't want the project to drive you out of your home," he said.

"Oh, I'm very glad you're doing this. I've thought for a long time that your living room could use a little more punch."

"You never said anything."

"It's not my place, dear."

Ethan felt his frustration level rise. Would he ever understand women? Probably not.

"When are you leaving?"

"In the morning." She paused from folding her shorts and tops. "You know, talking to Sylvia made me realize what a drastic step Robin took in canceling her wedding. She must have been very sure of her decision."

Ethan went to the refrigerator and grabbed a beer. "Why do you say that?"

"Just think about how much would have been involved in a society wedding like the one she must have planned. The florist, the caterer, the dressmaker, the entertainment. Then she had to arrange to return hundreds of gifts. I imagine she was absolutely exhausted when she left Houston to stay here."

"I suppose," he said, frowning at the suddenly bitter taste of the brew.

"Of course I'm right! Just think of that poor young woman, trying to graciously explain over and over why she was backing out of a match with a young man who seemed to be perfect. All without the support of her family or her fiancé."

Aunt Bess had painted a pretty grim picture of Robin's life right before moving here. But was it accurate? He thought back on what Robin had told him. She'd focused on the positive aspect of not marrying the wrong person. Since Robin obviously came from a wealthy family, he'd assumed her life was a breeze. But did he really know much about her?

"Well," Aunt Bess said, interrupting his thoughts, "I'd better get these clothes into the suitcase."

"Sure," he responded automatically, unwilling to stop thinking about Robin now that his aunt had so clearly described Robin's personal pain. Brow furrowed, he leaned against the counter and dangled his forgotten beer, wondering if he'd ever get Robin out of his mind.

ETHAN PULLED TO A STOP in front of the Franklin house, unsure of the reception he'd receive inside. Robin was apparently home, because her sporty red coupe was parked beside the house. She would no doubt be curious about this visit, but she might also be cool toward him. The question he wanted answered was whether her eyes would light up briefly before she schooled her face into a calm facade. Before she gave him a polite, phony smile.

Robin probably thought she was good at hiding her emotions, but she hadn't dealt with an FBI-trained officer before. He'd always been good at reading suspects.

At the moment, he suspected she'd stolen his heart when he wasn't looking. Otherwise, he'd be able to exert self-control and get her out of his mind. He'd tried, but he hadn't been able to forget her soft brown eyes, kissable lips or brave demeanor.

She didn't answer until he'd rung the bell twice and knocked several times. When she did open the door, her eyes appeared puffy and her nose pink. She sniffled before greeting him with a simple "Hello, Ethan."

She sounded more resigned to seeing him than happy he was there. She seemed sad, and his heart flipped in his chest.

He wanted to wrap her in his arms and hold on tight. He wanted to know everything she was feeling. The realization was fearsome.

"What's wrong?" he asked gently, taking one step closer.

"Nothing." She sniffed once more. "I'm just working on a wreath. All the dried flowers and moss and…everything makes me sniffle."

"You look like you've been doing more than sniffling."

She wouldn't meet his eyes. She wasn't about to

admit a weakness, which he could understand. She'd been through so much with her family and friends, topped off by moving to a town where she didn't know anyone but a meddling older lady and a confused cop.

"What can I do for you?"

"I just wanted to see you. Can I come in?"

She stepped out of the doorway. "Of course. Did you have a question about anything I'm doing at your house?" She pulled a tissue from her pocket and patted her eyes and nose.

"No, I'm sure everything is fine. I got your note about finding tables."

She walked to the couch and gestured for him to take a seat. He thought she looked tired, like maybe she wasn't sleeping well. He wanted to pull her into his arms, press her head against his shoulder and offer comfort.

"Can I get you something to drink? I still have the beer in the refrigerator from the night you came to dinner."

"No, I'm fine."

"So, what can I do for you?"

He twisted so he could rest his arm along the back of the couch. "I've missed you, Robin."

He watched her carefully. She blinked her slightly puffy eyes. The pink color on her pixieish nose intensified. He could practically see tears in her eyes.

"Robin, don't cry."

"I'm not crying," she stated, her voice shaky. "It's the moss and the dried flowers."

"Of course it is," he said, slipping closer. "So if I were to take you in my arms right now, that wouldn't cause any sort of reaction from you."

"I didn't say that." Her lower lip trembled as she stared at his with luminous, big brown eyes.

His heart beat faster, until he was certain she could see the pounding beneath his shirt. Something soft and needy unfurled inside his chest, and he knew he'd crossed a line when he'd entered her house this evening.

"Why don't we find out?" Before she could protest, he pulled her close against his chest.

"Those darn allergies can be pretty rough," he murmured against her soft, sweet-scented hair.

She nodded and settled more closely against him.

"Especially when you're all alone," he added softly.

A tiny whimper escaped her.

"It's okay, sweetheart. Go ahead and cry if it will make you feel better."

She shook her head ever so slightly.

"Why not?"

"Because it won't do any good," she said against his shirt front, her breath hot and moist through the cotton fabric.

"You might feel better."

"I don't think so. I think I'll still be here, away from my family and friends, and you'll still say you don't want to get involved."

"Maybe I changed my mind."

She punched his arm. "Darn it, Ethan Parker, you can't keep changing your mind. You can't be polite and aloof in the grocery and the restaurant, then come over here and look like you want more than a professional relationship. I don't know what you want! You're driving me crazy."

He smiled as he rested his cheek against her hair. "I know. I'm sorry."

She sighed, pressing more hot, moist air through his shirt. His pulse rate jumped again. Good thing she wasn't sitting across his lap or she'd be acutely aware of how much he wanted her...here, now.

"Ethan, I miss my life. I want to have lunch with my girlfriends. I want to develop new clients. I want to have Sunday dinner with my parents."

"I know you do." He pulled back a little to see her face, tracing the track of a tear with his fingertip. "You talked to Sylvia today, didn't you."

Robin nodded and sniffed. "She told me Bess was coming for a visit, and all I felt was jealousy." She winced and closed her eyes, as though she were experiencing actual pain. "Can you believe I was jealous of your dear aunt because she got to go to Houston and I have to stay here?"

He gripped her arms and looked into her eyes. "Sweetheart, you don't have to stay here. You made a decision to get out of Houston for a while. You agreed to house-sit, of course, but that doesn't mean you can't go back to see your family and friends."

She shook her head again. "I'm just not ready to face them yet."

"Why? You haven't done anything to be ashamed of."

"That's easy for you to say. You're not the one who did the walking out."

"No, but coming to your senses is no crime. If it were, I'd have to lock myself up."

She tilted her head in that adorable way. "What do you mean?"

"I mean that I've come to some realizations of my own lately, thanks to you. And also to my aunt, who pointed out a few facts to me before she left."

"Like what?"

"Like what a big deal it was for you to cancel your wedding." He smoothed a strand of her silky hair behind her ear. "Having never been rich, I couldn't imagine what that involved. When Monica was planning the wedding in Dallas, I got involved just a little. She'd ask my preferences on things like flowers and the reception menu, but basically it was a small affair for our immediate family and friends."

"Weddings should just be for two people, and those who love them."

"You're right, but I know they get out of hand. The second wedding was also small, but Belinda planned the whole thing. She was—is—a very traditional woman," he explained, hoping Robin would understand why he hadn't sympathized with her situation. "The difference was the attendance of so many people from Ranger Springs—people I worked with and served on a daily basis. Standing there at the altar with them watching, then coming to the realization that there would be no wedding, was more than embarrassing. I wanted to disappear into the floor. I wanted to hit something. I'd never felt so helpless in my life.''

Robin nodded. ''I felt helpless to stop the momentum of my wedding. Once the announcement was in the paper, I didn't have time to stop and think about what I was doing. I was comfortable with Gig in the sense that our families were close, our friends were mostly the same and our goals seemed to be similar. I just never realized how important a loving relationship was to me, nor did I realize how often Gig pushed me away when I tried to get close, until he accused me of smothering him.''

''I was the opposite. I didn't want to look too close. I think all along that I knew, deep down inside, that I wasn't ready to get married.''

''Oh, I still want it all,'' she said with fervor, ''but next time, I'm going in with both eyes open. I'm not going to pretend everything will be fine just because I make all the right decisions on silver patterns and caterers. I'm going to focus on what's in my heart, not what's presented for everyone else's benefit.''

''Good for you.'' He smiled in agreement at her heartfelt belief. But a part of him realized she was talking about some future, unnamed man she'd love. He didn't want to think of Robin with some-one else. He wanted her here, with him, so they could fully explore their feelings for each other.

"Next time, I'm going to make sure I get it right, because I quite frankly cannot afford another mis-take."

"What do you mean?"

"I felt so bad about the expense I caused every-one that I paid back my bridesmaids for their dresses and shoes, and I used the rest of my savings account to reimburse my parents for all the lost de-posits."

"With a wedding as large as you must have planned, I'm sure that was a pretty penny."

"That's one reason I'm house-sitting in Ranger Springs rather than lounging along the Mediterra-nean sipping champagne," she said with a forced chuckle. Her attempt to make light of her situation fell flat.

"What you did was honorable."

"Oh, I know money can't compensate for every-thing, but I tried my best to pay back what I could. And I apologized like crazy, but I could still tell my parents and friends didn't understand or agree with my decision."

"No one else can know what's right for you."

"I realize that now. I just needed a little distance from everyone. I was so tired of looking into their eyes and seeing questions about my judgment, even my sanity."

"They'll come around," he said, rubbing her

shoulder in a consoling way. "They need time, too."

"I know. That's the last gift I gave to all of us—time apart."

She hadn't talked about her current feelings for the man she'd left behind in Houston, and that did bother Ethan on some basic level. Before he went any farther in their relationship, he needed to know. "Robin, do you think you'll ever go back to Gig?"

"No," she said adamantly. "At some point I suppose I'll see him. I'll try to explain, to apologize, once more."

"You're dreading that, aren't you."

"Absolutely," she said. "Don't you think your former fiancées would feel uncomfortable around you?"

"I suppose, but maybe that's because I never did tell them I understood why they couldn't go through with the wedding."

"You really aren't angry with them anymore?"

"Not angry—although I have to admit to some irritation that they had such lousy timing in telling me they wanted to break up," he said, smiling as he tried to inject a little humor into their conversation. "But maybe you're right. Maybe I need to tell them I finally understand."

Robin smiled. "I just hope Gig will be able to feel more charitable about me in the future."

"I think he will. He'll find someone else. Oh, he might make you out to be the bad guy to his friends and family, but my guess is that any true feelings of anger won't be there unless he was truly, madly in love with you.''

"You obviously don't know Gig,'' Robin joked.

Ethan chuckled. He was glad she could joke about the breakup. It had taken him two years to get to that point.

He sobered as he looked into her luminous eyes. Something was going on between them, something he didn't understand yet. But he was determined to be honest with her and himself from now on.

"I don't know how much this means to you, but I'm really proud of you, Robin Cummings."

Chapter Thirteen

Robin felt as if a weight had been lifted from her shoulders, after telling Ethan more about the wedding that would have taken place today. Yes, if she'd gone through with the ceremony, tonight she'd be sipping champagne at the River Oaks Country Club, wondering if everyone was having a good time, worrying that something would go wrong and become the topic of conversation for weeks to come. And later, she'd begin her honeymoon with Warren "Gig" Harrelson, Jr.

They'd make love, no doubt, although they hadn't been intimate in months. That part of the relationship had soured about the time wedding preparations began—which should have been her first clue something was wrong between them. She couldn't even imagine or remember making love. Not while she was sitting within the circle of Ethan's strong arms.

She leaned back a little to look at him. He was so different from every other man she'd known. Ethan was strong, confident, intelligent. He seemed so certain of his abilities. He knew where he wanted to spend the rest of his life.

He was also incredibly sexy, and now that she was no longer sniffling and feeling sorry for herself, she became acutely aware of his scent, his nearness and his blue, bedroom eyes.

"What are you thinking?" he asked gently.

"I was admiring how you're sure of your place in the world, and of your goals."

"I've had a little more time to think about what I wanted."

She dismissed his answer. She knew he was only three years older than her, based on his college diploma, framed and hanging in the hallway, and on what Bess had told her. "I'm not sure time is the key."

He shrugged. "Then maybe it's the circumstances. Who we meet, what we know. I don't think there's a simple answer, but I'll make you a bet— I think you'll know what you want by the end of the summer."

"You think?"

He traced a finger along her cheek, sending shivers down her spine. "I do."

"And what are we betting?" She looked into his eyes. Blue was considered a cool color, but at the moment, Ethan's eyes burned as hot as molten lava.

He leaned closer, until she felt his warm breath on her mouth. "Why don't we decide later, after we know each other a little better?"

"How much better?" she whispered, her heart racing.

"A lot better," he said as his mouth hovered just out of reach. She wanted to reach up, claim the kiss she yearned to share, but she had to tell Ethan something first.

"Tonight was to be my wedding night," Robin whispered against his lips.

Ethan froze for just a moment. She leaned back to see his eyes, still burning hot. What was he thinking? She hoped he wasn't thinking of Gig or what might have been. But then Ethan's lids lowered, his mouth descended, and she was lost in a wild kiss that took her breath away.

When they'd kissed before, she'd known he was holding himself back. Tonight, she sensed he was letting go. A wild, exciting passion pulsed between them. His hands molded her to him, while his lips teased and tasted. If he was moving fast, she didn't care. She wanted him too much to keep any desire in reserve.

"Ethan," she whispered, as his kisses continued down her neck. With one hand he pushed her cotton knit top aside; with his mouth he drove her crazy with desire. How did he know the point where her shoulder met her neck was one of the most sensitive spots? At the moment, she didn't care how or why Ethan seemed to know everything about her. She simply wanted to seize the moment, share pleasure with him and create new memories.

His hand cupped her breast, his fingers searched

and found her sensitive tip. Robin moaned as she sank into the cushions of the couch. Feeling his weight on top of her, his leg pressing between hers, seemed right and natural. And oh, so exciting.

She wasn't worried about whether he'd respect her in the morning; she knew Ethan held women in the highest regard, and she believed he admired her for more than one reason. He hadn't wanted a temporary affair; neither did she.

She didn't know why this incredible passion was happening now. But she wanted this night with Ethan more than she wanted a future of regrets.

"Robin," he murmured against her throat, "I want to make love to you. But if you don't want me, tell me now."

"I do want you." She pulled his head up and kissed him hotly, her mouth devouring him. She tasted him thoroughly, then lightly stroked his bottom lip with her teeth. "I want you so much."

Ethan responded with a hiss of breath and a tightening of his hands on her hips and waist. "Let's get someplace more comfortable. Even with you stretched out on top, this couch is prettier than it is comfortable."

"Gee," she said, nibbling on his earlobe, "I hadn't noticed."

Ethan chuckled as he disengaged his arms and legs and struggled to his feet. His short hair looked as though it had been plowed in furrows, and his shirt was pulled loose from his jeans. Had she done that? The impressive bulge beneath his zipper spoke volumes about how much he wanted her, too.

The knowledge that she was responsible caused a secret smile she couldn't suppress.

He reached down and pulled her to her feet, then scooped her into his arms.

"Ethan!"

"You were to be a bride tonight," he said in a deep, sexy voice. "Let's create our own fantasy."

She felt tears threaten again, but this time they were tears of joy. She blinked them away and buried her face in his neck. "Down the hall and to the right," she whispered.

He carried her easily, as though unaware of her weight. One of Ethan's most admirable traits was his ability to focus on his goal: in this case, getting her to the bedroom as quickly as possible. Fine with her. She wanted to strip his shirt from his broad shoulders, pull him down on that queen-size bed and make love to him until they were both exhausted.

But would one night in his arms be enough?

As he maneuvered through the doorway, she pushed thoughts of the future from her mind. She wouldn't ask for commitment or explanation. She wouldn't press for more than he felt comfortable giving. She wouldn't expect more than a wonderful, passionate night…a wild, summer affair.

Ethan lay her down on the mattress in the same manner she might use to arrange an antique doll of delicate porcelain and lace. She could see his face in the light from the hallway, his expression both tender and hot.

He had started this fantasy, and she was more than willing to participate. Her shorts and top didn't resemble a bridal ensemble, but she could pretend.

"Would you like me to undress for you?" she whispered.

He nodded, his eyes full of desire as he eased onto the mattress.

Her fingers made slow work of the buttons down the front of her knit top, then she pulled it apart, revealing her thin, lacy bra. Thank heavens she'd chosen something sexy over functional earlier today. She could tell by the way Ethan was watching, by his rapid breathing, that he appreciated the choice, too.

"Do you remember what you said before about not being the most exciting man?"

He nodded, his eyes hot and focused on her face as she changed his attention from what she was doing to what she was saying.

"You're the sexiest, most exciting man I've ever known," she said softly, wiggling her shoulders free of the sweater.

He shuddered, but said nothing.

She moved to the waistband of her shorts, loosening the button, lowering the zipper. Looking up at Ethan, she said, "Help me."

His large hands skimmed up her legs, molding over her thighs and hips, before grasping the shorts and pulling them easily from her trembling body.

Seduction was powerful, she realized. She'd never done anything this blatantly sexual, but her desires, her actions, seemed natural with Ethan.

He leaned forward on arms braced on either side of her. He claimed her lips, his tongue stroking until she arched from the mattress. But she wasn't finished with this fantasy, and if he kept kissing her, she'd melt into a wax puddle on this comforter.

Breaking the kiss, she said, "Your turn." She propped herself up on her elbows and shook her hair back from her shoulders.

Ethan grinned as though she'd just given him a dare. He didn't need any bump-and-grind music to rival a Chippendale dancer. With skill and speed, he eased off the mattress and opened his khaki shirt, pulling it wide to expose his smooth, broad chest. He made equally short work of the button and zipper of his jeans, then slowed as he pulled his shirt free.

The night eased into slow motion as he revealed more and more flesh and muscle. He looked so good. Solid and strong. Confident and skilled. His shirt dropped to the floor. His jeans gaped open.

Robin licked her lips. "To serve and protect, right?"

"Absolutely."

"So I assume you have some protection?"

He pulled some packets from his pocket and tossed them on the bed. "These seemed like a good idea when I left the house tonight."

"For me."

"For us," he said, before dropping to the bed.

She watched impatiently as he pulled off boots and socks, then stood again. With a wicked, hot smile, he peeled off his jeans and briefs in one motion.

The dim light of the hall didn't do him justice. At some future date, she'd like to explore all of him in great detail. At the moment, he was much too far away.

She dropped back on the bed and opened her arms. He needed no further encouragement, and stretched out beside her. His warm, capable hands explored her through the thin bra and panties, then he showed he was as good at removing her underwear as he was at stripping off his own. While her heart beat wildly and she grew damp with desire, he pulled her against his hot, smooth flesh.

"Ethan, this is so good," she whispered.

He kissed her lips, her neck, her breasts. He would have lingered, but she needed him now. With low murmurs and moans, she let him know she was ready. Still, he hesitated…until she ripped open a packet with her teeth and sheathed him with shaking hands.

"Now," she said, and he complied, entering her slowly so she felt fully, completely, claimed. And then he kissed her and began to move, and she was lost to a passion so sweet she nearly wept. Ethan was around her, inside her, and as stars burst behind her closed eyes, everything seemed right in her world for the first time ever.

She knew where she belonged.

SUNDAY FOLLOWED in a haze of passion and discovery. Robin put on enough clothes to run to the mailbox at the end of the driveway. The paper was delivered there, in a quaint metal cylinder marked *Springs Gazette*. She jogged back to the house, smiling in pure joy at the glorious day, the incredible night and the wonderful man waiting for her inside.

At some time last night, he'd moved his Bronco around back so it couldn't be viewed from the road. Ethan was responsible and thoughtful—two traits that made him special.

He met her with a cup of fresh coffee and a kiss. Then she settled on the couch, with him on the floor by her, reading both the local paper and the *Austin Statesman* as the morning passed in a sunny blur. Occasionally, he would reach up to kiss her fingertips or stroke her leg, the gestures affectionate rather than blatantly sexual.

And he fixed breakfast—with her limited help— as his eyes grew hooded and his secret smile told her he was ready for more than pancakes and sausage. He wanted her, and the knowledge filled her with an anticipation and excitement she'd never before experienced.

They slept the afternoon away, until hunger forced them again from bed. Robin made sandwiches, and as they huddled together in the breakfast nook and shared potato chips, Robin told him more about her life in Houston. Her career. Why she loved making homes the places where people were happy and comfortable in their surroundings.

She realized that she'd been creating places where others would feel like they belonged, just as she'd always wished she belonged in her parents' lives, in their home. The realization brought tears to her eyes—happy tears, she told Ethan—and he kissed them away.

The one issue they never discussed was the future, which was probably for the best. The weekend was magic, a honeymoon of sorts during which they satisfied the desire, yet never totally quenched the hunger. What that meant, Robin wasn't sure. All she knew was that she wanted to repeat their time together again and again until she was sure of herself, of her feelings and of the future in his arms.

ETHAN AWOKE to the sounds of squirrels chattering in the trees and a cardinal calling his mate. *Mate.* His arm tightened around the warm, trusting woman snuggled beside him. Robin slept on her side, her hand on his chest, as though she wanted to feel the beat of his heart all night long.

If he lay here beside her much longer, his pulse would be racing and Robin wouldn't get her much-needed rest. They'd kept each other up half the night, making love, then sneaking into the kitchen to eat ice cream from the container and giggling like children. There was nothing childish in what had followed, however. He grew hard as he remembered carrying her to bed again and making love to her slowly, sweetly, until they'd fallen into an exhausted sleep.

He'd never had a wedding night or a honeymoon, but he couldn't imagine a better one than the time he'd spent with Robin.

Aching and aroused, he wanted to wake her and test the newfound passion, but the pale sunlight filtering through the sheer curtains on her window reminded him he'd better get to work.

Besides, thinking about wedding nights and Robin together had a sobering effect. He needed to evaluate what had happened between them this weekend, and he knew he'd never be able to use his brain if he was naked in bed with her.

And the citizens of Ranger Springs awaited. He had duties to perform, meetings to attend. He'd never taken his job as chief of police lightly. He loved this town and his position.

Ethan turned to look at the woman beside him. And what did he feel for her? Was it true love, or something more fleeting? He'd suspected for over a week that she could steal his heart. Is that what had happened this weekend? He wasn't sure how he could tell, but like any good cop, he had his suspicions.

She'd claimed Saturday night that he was exciting. He'd believed her then, but in the light of day, he knew he needed to understand his feelings before acting on his desires. Robin also needed a little time, he imagined, to be certain of her feelings. He didn't believe he'd been a substitute groom on what would have been her honeymoon, but she'd needed to be sure.

Steeling himself to leave her, he eased back the sheet and slid to the side of the bed. She immediately stirred and grumbled in her sleep. Ethan smiled despite his confused state of emotions. Robin looked so adorably rumpled, with her tangled hair, pursed and kissable lips and tiny frown lines in her forehead. He'd love to come back to bed, just so she'd smile and go to sleep once more—but he couldn't.

He stood, noticing the air-conditioning hadn't done a thing to reduce his desire for her. Perhaps he'd take a quick, cold shower before getting dressed.

"Ethan?"

Keeping his back to the bed, he bent down to retrieve his jeans and briefs. "Go back to sleep, sweetheart. I've got to get to work."

"Work?"

He found his briefs and pulled them on. "You know—serve and protect. I'm on duty this morning."

He turned back to the bed once he had some clothes on. Robin's eyes were still closed, but she had a dreamy smile on her face. Thinking of how he'd tried his best to serve and protect her all night long, no doubt.

Yes, a cold shower was going to be necessary.

"Will you come back later?"

He thought of his schedule that day: meeting with the mayor over breakfast, reviewing applications for a new officer, visiting the day-care center that afternoon. Did he have anything planned later?

"Why are you frowning?"

Her eyes were open and she was looking at him in concern. "I was just thinking about my day." He pulled on his jeans to put another layer of clothes between them, since Robin's sheet had slipped below her wonderfully round, pink-tipped breasts. "I'll call you later, and we can make plans," he said, knowing if he didn't get out of here soon, he was going to miss that damn meeting— and maybe the rest of his day.

"Everything's okay?"

He leaned down and kissed her cheek. "Everything's wonderful. I'll call you later, okay?"

She settled back into the pillows. "All right."

"I'm going to use your shower, then I'll lock up on the way out, okay? You go back to sleep."

She nodded, already drifting off with a satisfied smile on her face.

He'd truly exhausted her, he thought with a mixture of guilt and masculine pride. He'd always heard that sex could be a bit awkward at first. Maybe so, but making *love*…now, that wasn't awkward at all with the right person.

Chapter Fourteen

So this was what making love was supposed to be, Robin thought as she awoke the second time that morning. She'd imagined, she'd hoped, but she'd never experienced anything so great. Ethan was an amazing man. An exciting man. Truly, genuinely gifted, she thought with a smile as she threw back the covers. The women who'd left him at the altar were idiots. If they'd known what they were missing, they'd make a beeline to his door this very instant.

When her feet hit the carpet, a sobering thought intruded. What if they did know? One would assume Ethan had made love to them—at least the first, long-term fiancée in Dallas. Had their lovemaking been this spectacular? Damn, but she wanted to know if what she and Ethan had experienced last night was as extraordinary for him as it was for her.

He sure had seemed to enjoy it, she thought, letting her mind drift lazily back to the moment when he'd joined her on this bed that first time. When he'd changed her entire perception of sex. When he'd shown her what love felt like.

Love? Was she certain that's what they were feeling? Or was she caught up in the moment? She couldn't know until she saw him again. She couldn't be sure until they made love once more.

She slumped on the side of the mattress. Was that fair? She needed to get some perspective, just as she'd needed to with Gig. She'd ignored thinking about their relationship, their engagement, until she'd run off to Ranger Springs. She'd vowed not to repeat her previous mistakes. That meant being open and honest with Ethan, telling him how she felt and showing him what she wanted.

She wanted him. Not just memories of this weekend. Not just a casual summer fling.

With renewed spirit, she pushed up from the bed. Naked, she walked into her bathroom, where a hint of Ethan's presence remained. She ran her hand over the folded, damp bath towel. She smiled as she noticed the way he'd left the toothpaste and water glass in nearly the same position she kept them. Just as she suspected, Ethan Parker was neat and orderly. He wouldn't be a difficult man to live with…if that was the direction he wanted to take their relationship.

She hoped he did. She prayed he was at least open to thinking about the future.

But first, she needed to put the remnants of her past behind her. For weeks she hadn't been able to face the thought of returning to Houston and seeing her friends and family, much less apologizing once more to Gig. Now she knew she had to do those things, and quickly, so she could get on with her life here.

She paused, her hand resting on the sink as the truth set in. *Here.* As in Ranger Springs. Could she move to a small town after living her entire life in Houston? Three weeks ago she would have said the idea was absurd. Now...well, now she believed she could be happy in this small town, as long as she had Ethan. The rest of the details—her career, family and friends—she could work out.

She had to know. She had to be sure, even though her instincts told her this place, this man, was exactly what she'd wanted all her life.

AN HOUR AND A HALF LATER, Robin pulled her coupe into a parking spot in front of the municipal building and hurried toward Ethan's office. She wanted to see him, even if she couldn't touch him. Just to know if his eyes lit up when he faced her. If he wanted to reach for her, even though he shouldn't. That excitement fueled such energy that she barely kept herself from skipping into the police station.

"Hello...Susie, isn't it?" she greeted the receptionist.

"Hi, Miss Cummings. How are you?"

"Fine. Is Chief Parker in?"

"He's at lunch. I think he went to the café in town."

"Oh." Robin hadn't realized this was the noon hour. She'd been running on adrenaline all morning. "I'm a little hungry myself. I think I'll try to find him there."

"Okay. Should I tell him you came by if he calls in?"

"That would be great. Thanks, Susie."

"Sure, no problem. Say, how is your decorating project coming along?"

Decorating. She'd completely forgotten about that in the last sixteen or seventeen hours. She grinned. "I got a little sidetracked, but I'll be back working on it in a couple of days."

"I think that's so neat. I'd love to learn more about decorating."

"Maybe we can have lunch soon." Maybe she could teach a class at the community center. Maybe she could build a business here in Ranger Springs.

"I'd like that a lot. See you later, Miss Cummings."

"Please, call me Robin," she said with a wave as she hurried to her car.

But when she got to the café, she discovered Ethan wasn't there.

Disappointed, she paused for a moment to decide what to do next. Then her stomach growled, and she remembered she hadn't eaten all day…despite having expended a huge number of calories last night. With a sigh and a smile, she headed for Gina Mae's booth.

An hour later, her tummy full, she returned to

Ethan's office—only to discover she'd just missed him.

"He had a call to herd up a bunch of emus," Susie informed her.

"Eth—er, Chief Parker is out herding birds?" she asked incredulously.

"Yeah, kind of crazy, isn't it? You see, a few years ago emus were going to be the hot thing. Lots of people invested in breeding pairs with the hope of getting rich. But the market for emu products never took off, and people were stuck with these herds they couldn't afford to feed. Every now and then, someone just turns the birds loose to fend for themselves."

"That's terrible."

"Yes, especially because they're so stupid. They walk right out into the road, which causes accidents. Whenever we have a report of roving birds, Chief Parker sends as many officers as possible out to round them up."

"Interesting. So, I don't suppose you have any idea when he'll be back."

"No, there's no way to tell." Susie looked at her curiously. "Would you like to leave him a message?"

"Yes, I think that would be best." She really, really wanted to see him, but she couldn't insist he leave a bunch of helpless, hungry, stupid birds to get flattened by a big truck, while she gazed into his eyes.

Susie handed her a yellow pad, pen and envelope. "Just take your time."

She glanced at her watch. If she hurried, she'd still get back to Houston before the heaviest rush-hour traffic. "Thanks."

As quickly as possible, she wrote a note to Ethan, then printed "personal" on the envelope in plain block letters. She didn't want anyone reading her message to him. He'd get it sometime today, then he could call her tonight at her condo. They had a lot of things to discuss, but most would have to wait until she could be back in his arms again.

ETHAN WAS SO HOT and tired, he went directly home after rounding up the last frightened, hungry bird. They'd taken the emus to the 4-H fairgrounds where they could be safely contained, fed and watered until the judge decided what to do with them.

Ethan wouldn't have been so tired if he'd gotten a decent night's sleep last night, but he wasn't complaining. He wouldn't trade the experience of making love with Robin for a hundred nights of rest. Or even a lifetime of rest, he thought as he eased his boots off his aching feet. He was pretty sure this time he'd fallen hard and fast. The rest of the details could be worked out later—he sincerely hoped.

He needed another shower, this time hot and long, and then he'd phone Robin. He imagined her curled up on the couch, maybe sipping a glass of wine, waiting for his call. If he hurried, he could be at the Franklin house in forty-five minutes. They could be between the sheets in fifty.

But fifteen minutes later, after a shower, he listened as the telephone rang and rang. Robin didn't pick up; the answering machine finally engaged. Her voice said simply that she wasn't available, and to leave a message.

"Robin, this is Ethan. I just got off work. Call me when you get in. I'm really looking forward to seeing you again."

He finished getting dressed, then tried the number again. Still no answer. Frowning, he grabbed a beer from the refrigerator and settled onto his ugly couch, which had yet to be replaced. Across the room, a fresh coat of terra-cotta paint graced the dining room thanks to the painter Robin had hired. The man had done the job during the day so he didn't interfere with Ethan's schedule. The fireplace looked very different in a warm golden-beige rather than the natural pinkish-tan color of the bricks he was accustomed to. Robin had started the project in earnest a few days ago, but where was she now? He wished he had her cell phone number. He was sure she owned one, but he'd never had occasion to ask.

"Robin, where are you?" he asked the silent, empty house. Scowling, he clicked on the remote control and settled in to watch a baseball game.

An hour later, he couldn't sit still. He turned off the television and pushed up from the recliner, where he'd moved to when he'd realized he was sitting on the couch because he'd sat there with *her*. He tried calling her again, but there was still no answer. Frustrated, he grabbed his keys. He'd drive to her place and see if her car was in the drive. She could have had an accident, after all. Maybe she'd fallen in the shower.

The idea of Robin injured spurred him on, and within a minute, he was driving way too fast down the road toward the woman who'd captured his heart.

Her car wasn't in the drive or the garage. The house was closed up tightly. With the key he'd used that morning to lock up, he let himself inside.

"Robin," he called out.

No answer. He strode through the house, taking in the tidy appearance of each room. The breakfast area was cleared of dishes, and the Sunday paper they'd shared was in the trash. Even the old-fashioned, white-iron bed where they'd made love so sweetly, so many times, was neatly made with a floral comforter and lots of lacy pillows. He hadn't even noticed the furnishings last night.

None of Robin's things seemed to be out of place, but he really couldn't tell much because he wasn't sure what he was looking for. Not too many cosmetics were in the bathroom, but perhaps she simply didn't use a large variety. However, one clue was the lack of standard toiletries. He didn't see deodorant, shampoo or a woman's razor.

Could she have packed and left? But why, after the weekend? They'd been great together. He'd left with the pledge to call her later, and she'd seemed fine with his promise.

Why would she have left? Where would she go?

"Not back to Gig," he growled. No, Robin hadn't given any indication she wanted to get back together with her former fiancé. As far as Ethan knew, she didn't have any other friends around the area. Which left Houston.

Surely she hadn't run back to Houston after two nights in his arms. Surely he hadn't misread her reactions so completely. If he had, he was just about the worst FBI-trained lawman in Texas.

If anyone knew where Robin was, he felt her great-aunt Sylvia would. Unfortunately, he couldn't remember Sylvia's last name. Ethan sped back to his house to search the address book his aunt kept by the phone in the kitchen. Letting out an impatient sigh, he began with *A* and started looking for Robin's aunt.

His sense of anxiety grew with each passing minute. Robin wasn't the type of person to just up and leave, especially after a night like last night.

Everything had been perfect, hadn't it? He tried to recall anything that might have upset her, but couldn't come up with any clues.

Finally! Sylvia Murphy with a Houston area code. He punched the numbers into the wall phone, then drummed his fingers along the door facing until someone answered.

"Dammit," he cursed when the answering machine kicked in. He listened impatiently to the greeting, then left a message for Sylvia to call him collect as soon as she returned.

He grabbed a beer and slumped into his recliner. He'd thought he'd been frustrated before, when Robin was walking back and forth across his living room. He'd been wrong. Knowing now that she was out there somewhere and being unable to find her was the true definition of *frustration*. He just hoped he found her soon. He had something very important to tell Robin Cummings.

ETHAN PACED, wearing a path in the carpet between the living room and kitchen. Good thing he was getting his house redecorated, he thought, since he was about to ruin the flooring!

But the project would never be finished unless he found Robin. He hadn't seen her in more than twelve hours, and his anxiety grew each minute. He knew she'd contacted the station earlier in the day, but she hadn't left a message with the dispatcher. Ethan had insisted Ben look again for one of those pink message slips Susie always completed. Nothing. He'd even called Susie at home, just in case she knew something, but he only got her answering machine. Where was everyone on a Monday night?

After witnessing a dozen horrible crashes on the highways, or helping search for missing persons, he had a little experience with anxious situations. Right now, his imagination was shifting into overdrive. If he didn't hear from Sylvia, Bess or Robin within the next thirty minutes, he was going to put out an APB for a missing person.

He didn't approve of using his professional capacity to augment his personal life, but losing Robin qualified as a disaster. He'd do whatever necessary to find her quickly.

He'd need her driver's license number and license plate, he mentally cataloged. He could go down to the station to get that information, or he could—

The phone rang, interrupting his speculation. "Hello!"

"Good evening, Ethan. This is Bess."

"I know! Have you found Robin?"

"Why, yes, we have. She's with her parents."

"Why?"

"I have no idea. I haven't spoken to her yet."

"Give me the number, and I'll call her there."

His aunt recited Robin's phone number and address before adding, "Ethan, this doesn't sound like you at all."

He ran a hand through his hair. "I'm sorry, Aunt Bess, but I've been sick with worry since this afternoon. Robin had been in town looking for me earlier, then she left without seeing me or even leaving a message."

"That does sound rather irresponsible. Not like her at all." His aunt paused, then said, "What did you do to make her upset?"

"Me! I didn't do a thing."

''Hmm. Nothing's changed in your relationship, and suddenly she just runs off?''

Ethan felt his face grow warm. How could he explain to his beloved aunt that he and Robin had had the greatest weekend of lovemaking in history? After all, she'd accused him of getting less action than men in the retirement home. Now Bess was in Houston, staying with Robin's aunt, and he just couldn't tell two elderly ladies that Sylvia's great-niece and Bess's nephew were the hottest thing in bed since electric blankets.

''Ethan, are you still there?''

''Yes, Aunt Bess. All I can tell you is that Robin and I had a turning point in our relationship. I thought everything was wonderful.''

''And then she left.''

''Yes! Without a word.''

''She must have had her reasons. She's a very levelheaded young woman.''

''I know that. That's one of the things I lo—I admire about her.''

His aunt paused. ''I think Robin is talking about her wedding with her parents right now. I'm sure they had a lot of issues to discuss. I'm not sure what she's going to be doing tomorrow, but it wouldn't surprise me if she wanted to see that fiancé of hers.''

''That Gig fellow? She doesn't need to see him. They're finished.''

''Hmm. Well, I'm sure you're right. But tell me,

Ethan, did you confess to Robin how you felt about her?''

He thought back to all the time they'd spent together in the last 48 hours. Had he said the words? He was pretty sure he hadn't. They hadn't talked a lot. Maybe at the time he wasn't one-hundred percent sure how he felt. He was now.

''No, I don't think so, Aunt Bess, but that doesn't mean—''

''Ethan! A woman needs to hear these things. If she doesn't hear them from you, then...''

''Are you telling me that Robin is going to turn to some guy named Gig if he suddenly professes his love?''

''I'm not certain. I'm just saying that she broke off the engagement rather suddenly, and I'm sure there are a lot of unresolved feelings on everyone's part.''

Ethan scowled at the phone, greatly annoyed at his aunt for putting such ridiculous thoughts into words. Of course Robin wasn't interested in getting back together with her former fiancé. She'd realized she and Gig weren't right for each other. She'd grown beyond some frat jock who still used a childish nickname.

''Ethan, I think Sylvia needs to use the phone. Call me later when you decide what to do, all right?''

''Yes, Aunt Bess, I'll do that.''

What to do... He was, after all, a man of calm

and deliberate action. An officer of the law couldn't be rash and irresponsible.

But at the moment, he wanted to rope and hog-tie Gig Harrelson, then drag Robin across his saddle and ride off into the sunset.

Chapter Fifteen

Robin perched on the edge of her empire reproduction sofa, her fingers nervously fingering the mahogany detail that gave the piece such distinctive style. Gig was going to be here any moment, and she wasn't sure she was ready to see him. Maybe she should have suggested they meet in a public place, but she had been a bit concerned he might make a scene. If she'd stayed with her original plan of waiting two months before coming back to town, he would have had time to cool off. At three weeks—and just three days after their wedding was supposed to have taken place—she wasn't sure he would be receptive to her explanations.

And apology, she added. She had to tell him again how sorry she was to have put him and his family through this mess and expense.

The buzzer from Security sounded. Robin jumped up and answered.

"Yes, send him up," she said to the doorman. She smoothed the simple lavender sheath dress and praised her decision to wear flat sandals. She wouldn't have been able to pace nearly as well in heels.

Within a minute or so, a knock sounded. Smoothing her hair and dress one more time, she opened the door.

"Come in, Gig," she said as evenly as possible. "Thank you for coming over."

"You said it was important." He appeared irritated as he strode through the small foyer into the living room. He unbuttoned his suit coat and settled back on her couch. "I thought we'd said everything that needed to be said three weeks ago."

She poured them each a glass of iced tea, then set the drinks down on the coffee table. She settled back on a chair opposite the couch, not too close to Gig. "I suppose we did, at the time. But I've had a little time to think, and I—"

"Good God, you're not suggesting we get back together, are you?" he asked as he sat forward. "Because I've got to tell you that would be a really bad move."

Robin almost chuckled at the alarmed look on his handsome face. "No, Gig, I'm not suggesting that. I think we both came to the conclusion that we're not suited."

"That's one way to put it," he agreed, sitting back once more. "Besides, my parents would have a fit."

Yes, she supposed they would. And Gig did love to please his parents. "I'm sure mine would, too."

"So what's this about?"

She took a sip of her tea. "I came to a lot of realizations while I stayed in Ranger Springs. One thing I discovered was that I was still blaming you in some way for not being the type of man I needed. That was wrong of me, and I'm sorry."

"I don't know what you mean. If you're saying I'd make a lousy husband, I have to disagree. I thought we had a lot of things in common. Friends, interests, backgrounds."

"Yes, on the surface, we did. But what I meant was that I wanted—no, at the time, I needed—a man who would make me the center of his world. I was coming at the relationship from a somewhat childish perspective. All my life, I'd wanted my parents to put me above their social obligations and their own needs. When they didn't, Great-aunt Sylvia filled that void."

"I know you're really close to her."

"Yes, I am. She was wonderful to me when I was a child, and now as an adult. To tell you the truth, she's a lot warmer than my own mother."

Gig just shrugged. Obviously, all this "touchy feely" stuff was going right over his head.

"What I wanted to tell you, Gig, was that you weren't to blame for being exactly who you were. I just had unreasonable expectations of being a couple, and of marriage in general."

He frowned. "I never thought I'd done anything wrong."

Robin chuckled. "Then I guess you're one step ahead of me." She sobered, then added, "Another thing I realized is that if we'd gone ahead with the wedding, we would have made each other miserable. In the end, either I had to become more like my own mother, or you would have been besieged with requests from me to be more emotional. I don't think either one of those scenarios would have made us happy.''

He shrugged again. ''I suppose you're right. I just thought all along that you were one of us, Robin. I mean, you fit in so well.''

One of us. What an odd way for him to explain her position in the universe of their friends and family. Us and them. Perhaps that had been the problem all along: she'd been more like her less wealthy, warmer, more loving aunt than the social elite.

She smiled. ''I tried, Gig. I really did. Fitting in has always been important to me, but I think I've finally found someplace that really suits me.''

Gig stood up and buttoned his coat, signaling this meeting was over. ''I'd better get back to the office. Dad is having a department meeting this afternoon.''

And Big Gig wouldn't want his son to miss anything related to the family banking business, Robin silently added.

''I'm just glad we could sit down for a few minutes,'' she said aloud. ''I've really felt bad about canceling the wedding, but I think it was the best decision for us in the long run.''

''You're probably right. I've been seeing a little of Bitsy Monroe. You remember her, don't you?''

"The Monroe's younger daughter, right? I went to college with her sister."

"Right." Gig shrugged, then grinned. "She's kind of in the market, if you know what I mean."

Robin impulsively touched his arm, then gave him a big hug. He seemed startled, then hugged her back. He was big and solid, but he wasn't the man she loved.

"I'm really happy for you, Gig. I'm sure getting back—"

The door burst open. The opening was filled with about six feet two inches of enraged Texas lawman.

"Ethan!" She couldn't believe he was here, in Houston! Dressed in his uniform, sporting his badge and that big firearm he carried in a black leather holster, he looked downright dangerous. Not at all the gentle, loving man she'd known for weeks.

He looked exciting, intense, and she wanted him more than ever.

"Robin, I don't know what's going on, but I'm not going to stand by and let you reconcile with... him," he said, pointing to blond, wide-eyed Gig.

"What are you talking about?" she asked in a shaky voice.

"I don't care if he did hold you in his arms and promise he'd take you back. I'm not letting you go without a fight."

"What?" Gig asked, clearly confused.

"This is between me and Robin," Ethan stated, glaring at Gig.

"You're nuts," her former fiancé announced.

"Wait a minute!" she ordered, throwing up her hands. "Gig, please be quiet for a minute. Ethan, would you please tell me what you're saying."

Ethan stepped into the room, totally ignoring Gig. "I've been going crazy, thinking about you here in Houston with your friends and family, but especially—" he hooked a thumb in the general direction of her awestruck ex-fiancé "—with him."

"Ethan, you have the wrong idea."

"No, I don't, Robin. We're meant to be together. I don't care that our backgrounds are different, or that we both have a history of not making it to the altar. All that matters is how we feel about each other." He paused when he reached her, then took her shoulders in a gentle grip. "Robin, I love you."

Her mouth gaped open. "You do?"

"Yes. And I think you feel the same way about me."

"I do," she said quickly, reaching for his handsome face and framing his jaw with both hands.

A discreet cough sounded behind them. She'd forgotten Gig was in the room. At the moment, she still needed to explain her abrupt departure to Ethan. "I was going to tell you as soon as I got back to Ranger Springs, but I didn't want to leave it in my note."

"Note?"

"The note I left at your office."

He appeared totally baffled.

"On your desk, in a Ranger Springs Police De-

partment envelope with 'personal' written on it.''
She frowned. "You didn't get my note?"

"No. I haven't been to the office since I left to
herd the emus right after lunch. I called in several
times, but no one had seen a message slip from
you.''

"Herd emus?" Gig repeated.

They both ignored him. "Then how did you find
me?" Robin asked.

"I called Sylvia, then I talked to Bess. She gave
me your number and address. I wanted to call, but
I didn't know what to say, so I just got in my car
and drove to Houston.''

"Oh, Ethan." She hugged him close.

"I suppose congratulations are in order," Gig
said behind them.

Was he still in the room? Peering around Ethan,
Robin smiled at her ex. "Maybe. First, I have to
get a good offer.''

"An offer?" Ethan asked, ignoring Gig and fo-
cusing on her.

"A proposal, Officer Andy," Gig taunted.

He might not hold any grudges against *her* any
longer, but he obviously hadn't taken a shine to
Ethan, Robin noted.

"It's Ethan," Robin said quickly. "Police Chief
Ethan Parker.''

"Right. Well, I'm out of here. Good luck on getting the rest of it right.''

Ethan glared at him. Gig had the good grace to
leave without another comment.

"How did you get in this building?" she asked.

"Not right now. I think Gink is right. I have to make this official."

She hid her grin at Ethan's intentional mispronunciation of her ex's nickname. "Okay."

He glanced around the apartment. "Sit over here," he said, guiding her toward the couch.

She sat.

To her surprise, he pushed her ottoman-style coffee table out of the way and knelt on the plush red-and-gold oriental inspired rug. On one knee, he took her hands in his.

"I didn't plan very well for this. I don't have a ring with me, but I'd like us to pick one out later. Something you love, because your taste is a lot better than mine." He paused and swallowed. "That is, if you'll marry me."

She looked into his beautiful and intense blue eyes, her love for this strong, gentle man nearly overwhelming. "Are you sure?"

"I've never been more sure of anything. I want to spend my life with you. I want to raise our children in Ranger Springs. I want to find a way to compromise with your career. Most of all, I want to love you forever."

"Oh, Ethan," she whispered, tears welling in her eyes. "Yes. Yes to everything."

He took her in his arms, pulled her from the couch onto the floor and kissed her before she'd even settled into his lap. She'd always liked her oriental carpet, but at the moment, she truly appreciated its potential. As their kiss intensified, she envisioned pushing Ethan down onto the plush surface, ripping open his uniform shirt and having her way with him.

Memories of their lovemaking filled her with heat and need. She saw the reflection of her own desires in his eyes. His hands molded her, reaching for her aching breasts.

Another discreet cough sounded behind them.

Robin's eyes popped open. Ethan stiffened. Both turned to see what Gig could possibly want now.

But the scene that greeted them was right out of their teenage pasts.

Sylvia and Bess stood in the doorway, big smiles on their faces.

Robin dropped her head against Ethan's shoulder and whispered, "The first time I met Bess in the fast-food restaurant where you two were eating dinner, I felt like I was back in the junior high school cafeteria. Now I feel like I've been caught necking in the car."

"I'm sorry we interrupted, dear," Sylvia said, stepping into the condo.

Robin looked up and smiled. "Your timing is just great," she said with just a little bit of sarcasm.

"I know, I know." Sylvia tsked. "But your door was wide open."

Darn Gig. Didn't he have the sense to close a door when he left?

"We came to see if Ethan had arrived yet," Bess added.

"As you can see, Aunt Bess, I did come to Houston. It's a good thing you warned me what was up. I think I arrived in the nick of time."

"What are you talking about now?" Robin asked. "What warning?"

"Aunt Bess told me you might be getting back with your former fiancé. I wasn't about to lose you to ol' Gink, so I got here as soon as I could."

Robin turned to Bess. "Where in the world did you get the idea I wanted to reunite with Gig?"

The older ladies turned to each other, looking guilty. "We thought there was a possibility," Bess said weakly.

"A very slight possibility," Sylvia added.

"What! I never said anything about Gig except that I wanted to apologize and explain one more time."

"Then you two weren't really hugging when I walked in?" Ethan asked.

"No, of course not. I mean, it was a hug, but like a sister and brother. Gig already has his eyes set on Bitsy Monroe."

"That vacant-minded little—"

"Aunt Sylvia!"

She sniffed. "I'd say she and Warren will make a good couple."

Robin crossed her arms over her chest and narrowed her eyes. "Matchmaking again, Aunt Sylvia?"

"What?" She turned to look at Bess. "I don't know where she gets these ideas." Linking her arm with her friend's, Sylvia turned to leave. "I think we'd better leave these two alone."

She turned to leave. "This time, we'll shut the door. You never know who's going to walk in around here."

"You're right," Robin heard Bess say. "It's barely noon on a Tuesday, and there's more action here than in the retirement home!"

When Robin looked at Ethan's amused expression, she burst out laughing. Hugging and giggling like two fools, they fell to the rug, wrapped in each other's arms.

Ethan smoothed the hair back from her face with his two large, capable hands. "I think we're finally alone."

"I think you're right, although I won't promise for how long. Once my parents get wind of this, they might show up."

He teased her with a nibbling kiss. "Any more old suitors expected today?"

"No," she said, closing her eyes and savoring his touch, his weight, as she lay beneath him.

"No more urgent apologies to make?"

"No," she whispered against his lips.

"Then let's take advantage of the moment. We've been apart far too long."

"Absolutely." She nibbled on his lips and stroked his strong, solid back.

"And we're not going to be apart again, are we?"

"Not for long."

"And you'll live with me in Ranger Springs?"

"Yes." She wiggled against him, aching for his touch.

"Be my wife?"

"Yes."

"Have our babies?"

She stilled, then grinned. "Yes."

"I love you, Robin."

"I love you, too, Ethan. Now be quiet and show me how much you missed me. I have an idea this is the last good use I'm going to get for a red, black and gold oriental rug."

"You might be getting rid of the rug, sweetheart, but I'm here to stay."

Epilogue

A small-town wedding was different in several ways from a big-city event, Robin learned as she looked out the window at Bretford House. She'd been hidden from her soon-to-be-bridegroom's eyes in a small room used just for this purpose—and for the storage of additional napkins, tablecloths and Christmas decorations.

First, the ushers couldn't control the crowd. Second, everyone believed they should be in the planning. And third, she would still get suspicious stares until she made an honest man of their beloved police chief.

"It's almost time," Great-aunt Sylvia said as she carried the flower-adorned veil across the room.

Robin let the lace curtain fall back into place. "I hope it's not too hot outside."

"Everyone's dressed for the heat—except, of course, your mother. She simply wouldn't listen when Bess tried to talk her out of panty hose and high heels."

Robin smiled, remembering the look of horror on

her mother's face when trying to walk across the lawn earlier today, the spiky heels of her designer sandals sinking past the grass into the sandy soil. "She has her own opinion about what's a proper wedding for her daughter."

"Yes," Sylvia said, reaching up to kiss her cheek, "but you had the good sense not to listen."

Robin laughed. "How could I listen to her when half the town had already decided how I'd be getting married?"

"Nonsense," Bess said, entering the room and closing the door quickly, as if someone might try to gain a peek at the bride before the ceremony. "You could have put your foot down."

"I know, but I honestly enjoyed going along with the suggestions. This compromise is so much more appropriate for Ethan and me than a big church wedding in Houston."

"And much more fun," Sylvia said.

Robin smiled. She'd kept her flower girl and ring bearer from the first planned wedding, because her cousins' children were looking forward to participating. But she'd explained to her bridesmaids that she'd rather have them attend as friends than stand up beside her in the September heat. After cutting down the guest list to immediate family and very close friends, she had a bride's group that would just barely fit into the folding chairs on the lawn outside.

And the groom's side was full with Ethan's parents and family, a few friends from Dallas and many of the citizens of Ranger Springs. The town leaders and the regulars from the café were dabbing perspiration from their foreheads and no doubt gossiping away.

Those who couldn't fit into the chairs stood across the fence in back. The scene outside reminded Robin, in some ways, of a high school football game more than a wedding. But overall, she couldn't have asked for a better arrangement.

Life was certainly going to be different here than if she'd stayed in her own world. She'd sold her condo to Bess, who'd decided to move back to town to be near her friend. Robin's Nest, a design studio and antique mall, would be opening in late November in the abandoned theater. Ethan's house had almost completed its metamorphosis into a home with furnishings and colors they both agreed upon.

And they were getting married.

She looked around at two women she loved dearly, then out the window once more at the townspeople who had adopted her as one of their own. For the first time in her life, she knew she'd found the place she truly belonged, with the one man she loved with all her heart.

WHERE IN THE HECK was Robin?

Ethan shifted uncomfortably from one foot to the other, chafing in his gray tuxedo, impatient for the ceremony to be concluded so he could change clothes, get on with the party, and then start his honeymoon with his bride.

His dad patted him on the arm. "She'll be here in a minute, son."

His best man, Gray Phillips, a good friend from Dallas who had relocated to Ranger Springs that summer, moved closer and said, "This isn't going to be like the last time."

"I know that," Ethan replied testily.

He did know it deep in his heart, but he couldn't help recalling the two other times he'd stood alone in front of a preacher. At Robin's urging, he'd contacted both his former fiancées. They'd been reluctant to talk to him at first—especially Belinda, who suspected he wanted to yell at her. He hadn't, of course. Monica was a bit cooler, as she'd always been, until he'd explained he finally understood, thanks to the woman he was going to marry. He'd gotten congratulations from both women. They'd never be great friends, but at least he'd made the effort.

Now he was ready to move on. He wanted to see Robin walk down that aisle, and right this second wouldn't be too soon.

"You're not thinking happy thoughts," Gray whispered with just enough humor in his voice to make Ethan want to flatten him.

"If you want to be helpful, go find my bride. I'm melting out here."

"September is still summer in Texas," his dad

told him, as though someone who'd grown up here all his life needed reminding.

The music started, jolting him to awareness. Suddenly the birds stilled, the insect buzzing faded away and even the low conversation of the many guests halted. Under the spreading canopy of the live oak trees beside Bretford House, all eyes turned to the creamy carpet bordered by pots of white daisies. A tiny flower girl, dressed in sunny yellow, tossed rose petals across the carpet for Robin to walk across...*if* she ever did walk out of Bretford House, Ethan thought.

"Shouldn't she be coming out now?" he whispered urgently to his best man.

"The bridal march hasn't started yet. Be patient."

Easy for Gray to say. This wasn't *his* wedding. To be more precise, this wasn't the third time *he'd* almost gotten married. "Just wait, buddy. You'll be standing here one day."

"Sure I will. And pigs will fly."

Before Ethan could come up with a snappy reply, the music he recognized so well from his prior trips to the altar flowed from the organist's fingers like a powerful opiate through the summer day. The crowd sat straight and silent, appearing not to breath. He had to remind himself to inhale, exhale, as he watched the side doors to the restaurant.

And then she appeared, a vision in creamy lace and silk, holding tightly to the arm of her distinguished father. She looked nervous, Ethan thought.

Maybe she wasn't sure. Maybe she wouldn't be happy living in a small town with a quiet, down-to-earth police chief.

Then her gaze found him across the expanse of grass and flowers, carpet and guests and makeshift rows of chairs, and she smiled.

And it was the most beautiful smile he'd ever seen. His heart soared. His fears vanished.

He watched in awe and love as she neared him. The day, the wedding procession, even the music faded into the background. With a lump in his throat the size of Texas, he looped her arm through his and faced his bride.

"The third time's a charm," she whispered.

And he knew their lives would be wonderful from now until forever.

**Don't miss
an exciting opportunity
to save on the purchase of
Harlequin and Silhouette books!**

Buy any two Harlequin or
Silhouette books and save
$10.00 off future Harlequin
and Silhouette purchases

OR

buy any three
Harlequin or Silhouette books
and save **$20.00 off** future
Harlequin and Silhouette purchases.

**Watch for details
coming in October 2000!**

PHQ400

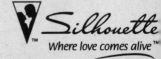

HARLEQUIN®

A M E R I C A N ✦ R O M A N C E®

A couple in love, a tender proposal,

a special walk down the aisle....

Sometimes, that isn't *quite* the way it happens!

However they get there, you can be sure these
couples will stay

HAPPILY
WEDDED
AFTER

**THE GROOM
CAME C.O.D.**
by Mollie Molay
August 2000

**WHO GETS TO
MARRY MAX?**
by Neesa Hart
September 2000

**SPECIAL ORDER
GROOM**
by Tina Leonard
October 2000

**THE MARRIAGE
PORTRAIT**
by Pamela Bauer
November 2000

Join Harlequin American Romance for these
extra-romantic trips to the altar!

Available at your favorite retail outlet.

HARLEQUIN®
Makes any time special ™

Visit us at www.eHarlequin.com.　　　　HARHWA

COMING NEXT MONTH

#845 WILD THING by Anne Stuart
He had no identity and no past, but what the silent mystery man did have was the body of a god. It was Dr. Elizabeth Holden's job to uncover his secrets, but could she succeed before her primal instincts got the best of her?

#846 SPECIAL ORDER GROOM by Tina Leonard
Happily Wedded After
Bridal salon owner Crystal Jennings would rather stick a straight pin in her eye than wear one of her own creations. But when her meddlesome family dared her to date the first man who walked into her store, she didn't expect it to be Mitch McStern—the one man who just might get her to walk down the aisle!

#847 OPEN IN NINE MONTHS by Leanna Wilson
Joy Chase was keeping a secret—a little nine-month secret—from handsome Sam McCall. And when she ran into the dashing single dad, could the romance-weary woman find a way to reveal her secret— without revealing her heart's desire?

#848 A LITTLE OFFICE ROMANCE by Michele Dunaway
Desperate for some quick cash, Julia Grayson agreed to pose as her best friend's brother's new temporary secretary. Yet working for the deliciously tempting Alex Ravenwood soon had Julia hoping for a permanent little office romance!

Visit us at www.eHarlequin.com